Prologue

The rain fell on Chicago like a thousand tiny needles, each one a whisper of the city's unforgiving nature. Inside the hidden cell of a forgotten industrial building, the rhythm of the storm was the only sound, a relentless drumming on the grime-streaked windowpane. The air, thick with the scent of damp concrete and stale cigarette smoke, was a fragile sanctuary that existed on borrowed time.

Agent Finn "Shadow" Kage stood by the window, a silhouette against the flickering neon of the city below. The scar on his knuckles, a jagged white line from a long-forgotten fight, was a ghost of his past, a testament to the life he had once lived—the life he was still living, in two separate, warring worlds. His gaze, sharp and observant as always, scanned the streets below, searching for a phantom threat that was always there, just beyond the edge of his perception. The scent of his alpha, a clean, sharp, dominant perfume, was a silent

THE AGENTS CONFESSION

Copyright © 2025 Clara Throne

alarm in the small room, a constant, low-level hum of suppressed rage and protective instinct.

On a narrow cot in the corner, Rhys Petrov was a small, quiet island in the storm. His pale skin, luminous in the dim light, and his brilliant blue eyes were a beacon in the darkness. He was a puzzle of contrasts: the gentle omega with a mind like a steel trap, the brilliant accountant whose meticulous work had built an empire he now wanted to burn. He was a survivor, a quiet, defiant force of nature, and in his belly, a soft, insistent flutter—a new life, a child that was both the final, beautiful culmination of their love and a ticking clock of unimaginable danger.

Their bond, a fragile, beautiful thing forged in a world of lies and manipulation, was the only truth that mattered. It was a secret, a crime, a defiant act of rebellion against a system that wanted to use them both and then discard them. Finn had spent his life playing a part, a faceless agent in a war he thought was righteous.

But with Rhys, the part had become the man. The mask had become his face.

The silence, a beautiful, terrifying thing, stretched between them. It was a language of unspoken fears and desperate hopes, a moment of peace before the final storm. Then, a new sound, the sharp, insistent vibration of a burner phone on the concrete, shattered the quiet. The low, guttural murmur of a voice, a cold, casual command, a voice that was both familiar and alien, echoed through the small, fragile room. A ghost in the machine, a final, definitive truth.

Finn's hand, a rough, calloused thing, moved to his gun. The mask, the agent, the protector, was gone. All that was left was a man, a father, a furious guardian who was about to lose everything. The two worlds, his duty and his love, had finally collided. And in the wreckage, there would be no going back.

Chapter 1

The Shadow and the Starlight

The rain-slicked streets of Chicago glittered ten stories below, a fractured mosaic of car headlights and neon signs. Inside the Petrov family's downtown office, a kingdom of muted grays and polished mahogany, the air was a world away from the city's frantic pulse. It was silent, sterile, scented faintly with the metallic tang of new ink and the dusty weight of old paper. Here, Agent Finn Kage was a ghost in the machine. He moved through the opulence as "Shadow," a quiet numbers man with an eidetic memory and a talent for dissecting the Petrovs' sprawling financial empire. His days were a monotonous cycle of numbers and lies, each interaction with Rhys, the family's unassuming omega accountant, a test of his resolve.

Finn sat hunched over a ledger, its pages as meticulously organized as the lies he lived. His gaze was a cold, hard thing, a predator's focus on a single piece of paper, a stark contrast to the unassuming accountant he pretended to be. His powerful alpha frame was softened by a deliberate slouch, a feigned carelessness that hid the coiled tension beneath. Yet, beneath the veneer of a mundane existence, the wolf paced. His gray eyes, usually as still as a winter lake, moved with a surgical precision, each sweep across the page a calculated search for the truth hidden within the deceit. He was at a crucial point in his mission, just days away from gathering the final piece of evidence needed to bring down the Petrovs, the last domino in a long, patient game.

Across the sprawling, dimly lit room, Rhys sat at his own desk, his fingers a blur of motion across a keyboard. The soft, cerulean glow of his monitor cast a halo around his silhouette, illuminating the delicate curve of his neck and the fine lines of his jaw. Rhys was a contradiction: a slight-framed omega who moved with the quiet confidence of a man who knew his own mind, a mind so brilliant it was almost a weapon. He was the only one in the entire operation who could keep up with Finn's meticulous pace, and the only one who seemed to see Finn for more than a faceless employee. Finn caught the flicker of Rhys's gaze from across the room, a brief, admiring glance that made an unfamiliar ache bloom in his chest. He quickly looked down, the ledger a shield against the quiet warmth that threatened to melt his carefully constructed facade. The scent of him, faint and distant, was a soft, calming blend of rain and sandalwood, a ghost on the air that Finn tried desperately to ignore.

Hours bled into minutes, the rhythmic drumming of rain against the immense glass windows now a steady downpour. The city outside, a beautiful, chaotic painting of shimmering gold and silver, was a world away from the suffocating silence within the office. The only sound was the hushed click of keys and the faint scratching of Finn's pen on paper. The late hour had chased everyone else out of the office, leaving them in a sea of encroaching darkness, two islands of illumination in an otherwise empty space.

Suddenly, Finn's fingers stalled. His gaze, once so certain, now flickered over a series of numbers. It was a discrepancy so small it was almost nonexistent—a single entry for a shipment of "construction materials" that was off by a fraction of a percent. The number was inconsequential, the kind of detail most people would chalk up to a typo and ignore. But not Finn. And not Rhys. Finn's jaw tightened, a muscle jumping in his cheek. He was growing weary of the charade, of the constant vigilance, of the cold, sterile reality of his life. He pushed the ledger away, the movement a silent, frustrated curse. He had to stay late, to re-examine the numbers, to ensure the integrity of his falsified accounts.

The scrape of a chair across the floor startled him. Finn looked up to see Rhys standing, his hands tucked in the pockets of his slacks, his posture a study in quiet hesitation. "You're still here," Rhys said, his voice a soft murmur that seemed to swallow the silence.

Finn nodded, a curt, formal gesture. "Something isn't adding up."

Rhys's brows furrowed in concentration. "Mind if I take a look?"

Before Finn could object, Rhys was moving, a fluid, graceful walk that felt both deliberate and unstudied. He crossed the space between their desks in a few silent steps, his presence a sudden, sharp intake of air in the quiet room. He leaned over Finn's desk, his attention focused on the numbers. He was so close that Finn could feel the heat radiating off him, could hear the faint, steady rhythm of his breathing. And then the scent hit him.

It was a scent Finn had come to associate with quiet nights and shared coffee—a soft, earthy blend of rain and sandalwood, a scent as comforting and real as a warm blanket. It washed over Finn, a wave of pure, unadulterated omega, and for a fleeting, terrifying moment, the carefully built walls of his alpha nature began to crumble. He found himself inhaling, a deep, involuntary breath that filled his lungs with the scent of Rhys, of home, of a life he couldn't have. He squeezed his eyes shut for a moment, the numbers on the page blurring into a meaningless mess. His heart, a traitorous thing, hammered a frantic rhythm against his ribs, a frantic, desperate drumbeat that screamed of an alpha's desire to protect, to claim, to hold.

"You're right," Rhys said, his voice a low murmur. His finger traced the line, his nail a pale crescent against the dark ink. "It's a rounding error, but it shouldn't be there." He leaned in closer, his shoulder brushing against Finn's arm, a fleeting touch that felt like a bolt of lightning. "The shipping manifest says it was ten thousand tons. The invoice says nine thousand, nine hundred and ninety-nine point five. The difference is negligible, but... it's a detail."

Finn's mind raced, not with the numbers, but with the sudden, overwhelming proximity of Rhys. He could feel the warmth of his skin, the gentle sway of his body as he moved. He could see the faint constellation of freckles that dusted his cheek, the long, dark lashes that framed his eyes. The world had shrunk to this moment, to the scent and the warmth of Rhys.

"It's a distraction," Finn said, the words forced from his throat. "A way to hide a bigger number." His mind, a cold, calculating machine, was already piecing it together, the small discrepancy leading to a much larger crime.

"Exactly," Rhys said, his voice filled with a quiet triumph. "A ghost number. A lie tucked away in plain sight." He looked up, his eyes, a deep, liquid brown, meeting Finn's. A smile, small and genuine, tugged at the corner of his lips. "You're good at this."

The compliment was a shock to Finn's system, a sudden, bright jolt of warmth that made his carefully guarded heart beat a frantic rhythm against his ribs. He felt a blush creep up his neck, a sensation so foreign he almost didn't recognize it. He pulled back, the movement sharp and deliberate, breaking the fragile tension between them.

"I'm just doing my job," he said, his voice gruff, his gaze dropping back to the ledger. He couldn't look at Rhys, couldn't risk letting him see the flicker of something he couldn't afford to feel.

"Still," Rhys said, his voice dropping to a whisper. "Everyone else would have missed it." He straightened, a small sigh escaping his lips. "It's late. You should go home."

"You too," Finn said, the words a forced formality. He didn't want him to leave. The thought of being alone in the sterile silence of this office, with only the numbers and the lies for company, was suddenly unbearable.

"I can't," Rhys said, a shadow crossing his face. "There's still so much to do."

"Let me help," Finn said, the offer spilling from his lips before he could stop it. The words hung in the air between them, a fragile bridge between their two separate worlds. He saw the surprise in Rhys's eyes, the small, hopeful flicker of light that bloomed there, and knew he had made a mistake. He was getting too close. He was letting his guard down. He was blurring the lines between his mission and his life, and that was a line he couldn't afford to cross.

But the look in Rhys's eyes, a look of pure, unadulterated gratitude, was a more powerful pull than any protocol.

"Thank you," Rhys said, the words a balm to the raw, exposed part of Finn's heart. He moved back to his desk, the silence settling between them once more, but this time, it was different. It was no longer the empty, suffocating silence of two strangers. It was the quiet, comfortable silence of two people working together, a shared space carved out of a world of lies.

Finn worked, his focus now split between the ledger and the quiet presence of Rhys. He watched as Rhys moved, a fluid, graceful dance of fingers and keys, his concentration a palpable thing. The scent of rain and sandalwood lingered in the air, a constant reminder of the fragile, dangerous connection that was forming between them. It was a connection built on nothing but late nights and shared coffee, a foundation of lies and a single, honest moment of recognition.

Hours bled into minutes, the rhythmic drumming of rain against the window now a steady downpour. The city lights outside blurred into a watercolor of shimmering gold and silver, a beautiful, chaotic painting of a world Finn was trying to destroy.

Suddenly, a loud bang from the hallway outside shattered the silence. Both men froze, their heads snapping up, their eyes meeting across the room. The sound was followed by the low murmur of voices, the sharp click of a key in the lock, and the slow creak of the office door. Finn's hand, a blur of motion, reached for the small, innocuous pen on his desk, his fingers wrapping around the cold steel of the hidden blade. He was an Alpha in the presence of an Omega, and his protective instincts screamed to life, a primal roar of warning.

The door swung open, revealing Dimitri Petrov, his face a mask of cold, controlled fury. His silver-streaked hair was plastered to his forehead with rain, and his expensive suit, a dark, tailored thing of beauty, was soaked through. His eyes, the color of a winter sky, swept the room, landing first on Rhys, then on Finn, and a slow, predatory smile spread across his face.

"Rhys," he said, his voice a low, dangerous growl. "I didn't expect to find you here. Working late?"

Rhys's body went rigid, his shoulders tensing. He didn't look at Dimitri, his gaze fixed on his monitor. "Yes, sir," he said, his voice a quiet murmur. "Just finishing up."

"And you," Dimitri said, his gaze shifting to Finn, his eyes narrowing. "Agent Kage. You're a diligent man." The compliment, Finn knew, was a thinly veiled threat. Dimitri was a man who saw diligence as a potential threat, a sign of ambition that needed to be kept in check.

"Just doing my job, sir," Finn said, his voice a monotone, his face a carefully constructed mask of disinterest. His hand, hidden from view, tightened around the pen, his knuckles turning white.

Dimitri stepped into the room, his presence filling the space with a suffocating, oppressive weight. The scent of a powerful, dominant alpha, a scent of old money and new blood, filled Finn's senses, a bitter, metallic tang that made his teeth ache. He felt the wolf inside him bristle, an instinctual reaction to a rival alpha, a threat. But he suppressed it, burying the feeling deep beneath layers of protocol and discipline.

"I need to speak with Rhys," Dimitri said, his gaze never leaving Finn. It was a command, a dismissal, a line drawn in the sand.

Finn looked at Rhys, a silent question passing between them. Rhys gave a small, almost imperceptible shake of his head, a plea for him to stay, to not leave him alone with Dimitri. But Finn knew he had no choice. He was a ghost in this machine, and ghosts didn't have a say in who they haunted.

He stood, his movements slow and deliberate. He gave a small, formal nod to Dimitri, and then, without a word, he walked out of the office, the click of the door closing behind him a final, heavy punctuation. He didn't look back, but he could feel the weight of Rhys's gaze on his back, a silent plea hanging in the air like a ghost of its own.

As he walked down the empty hallway, the low murmur of Dimitri's voice echoing behind the closed door, Finn's heart pounded a frantic, furious rhythm against his ribs. He felt a cold dread settle in his stomach, a feeling he hadn't experienced since his first mission. He had left Rhys alone with the monster, and the thought was a knife twisting in his gut.

He stopped at the end of the hallway, a dark corner where the shadows were thick and deep. He leaned against the cool wall, his eyes closed, his breathing coming in ragged gasps. He could still smell the rain and sandalwood, a ghost scent that clung to his clothes, a constant reminder of the fragile, dangerous connection that was forming between them. A connection he couldn't afford. A connection that was getting dangerously close to becoming something real, something he was supposed to destroy.

He pulled out his phone, his fingers hovering over a contact he hadn't used in months. He was violating protocol, breaking a rule he had sworn to uphold. But the thought of Rhys, of his scent, of the small, hopeful smile he had given him, was a more powerful force than any rule.

He typed out a message, his fingers clumsy and slow, the words a raw, unfiltered cry from his heart.

"Are you okay?"

He stared at the screen, the blue light illuminating his face in the dark of the car. He wasn't sure why he was doing this, why he was risking everything for a man he was supposed to be a ghost to. But he couldn't stop. He had to know. He had to hear his voice, or at least see a sign that he was safe.

The silence stretched, a long, agonizing moment of waiting. He held his breath, his heart pounding a frantic rhythm against his ribs. The world had shrunk to this single, terrifying moment, to the small, glowing screen in his hand.

And then, the phone vibrated. A single word, a single, blessed word, appeared on the screen, a beacon of hope in the darkness.

"Yes."

Finn let out a long, shuddering breath, the tension in his shoulders melting away. He wasn't sure what he had expected, what he had feared. But the single word was enough. It was a lifeline, a connection, a small, fragile thread of hope in the vast, dangerous web he was caught in.

He put the phone away, the image of Rhys's smile burned into his mind. He was getting too close. He was blurring the lines. He was losing himself in the charade, and that was a line he couldn't afford to cross. But as he sat there, in the dark of his car, with the scent of rain and sandalwood clinging to him, he knew. He was already across the line. He had already fallen.

The next morning, the office was a different place. The air, once thick with the sterile scent of new ink and old paper, now held a faint, floral aroma, a soft, sweet scent that made Finn's senses prickle. He looked up, his gaze sweeping the room. Rhys was already there, his head bent over a ledger, his fingers a blur of motion. He was wearing a different shirt, a light blue one that made his eyes seem even more liquid and deep.

He looked up, his eyes meeting Finn's. A small, shy smile touched his lips, and he gave a small, almost imperceptible nod. It was a silent greeting, a secret shared between the two of them, a secret that felt both dangerous and thrilling.

Finn gave a small nod in return, the gesture feeling clumsy and foreign. He looked away, his gaze falling back to the ledger in front of him. But he couldn't focus. The numbers, once a source of comfort and clarity, were now just a meaningless jumble of figures. All he could see was Rhys, all he could smell was the faint, floral scent that now clung to the air.

He was a ghost in this machine, an anachronism in this world of polished wood and hushed tones. But now, there was a ghost of something else. A ghost of a smile, a ghost of a touch, a ghost of a scent that clung to his clothes and his skin. He was a ghost, but he was no longer alone. He had a partner in this silent, dangerous dance, a partner he was getting dangerously close to falling in love with.

The following days were a blur of numbers and lies, the pretense of their shared work a thin veil over the growing tension between them. They were two poles, pulled together by an unseen, undeniable force. Finn was a predator, a wolf in sheep's clothing, and Rhys was his prey, a gentle lamb in the lion's den. The irony was a bitter taste in his mouth.

He had the final piece of evidence now, a single entry that would bring down the entire Petrov empire. It was a small, insignificant number, a ghost in the machine that only Rhys's genius would have caught, a number Finn had manipulated to be just so. It was a cruel, brilliant plan, a masterpiece of deceit, and the only thing he felt was a profound, suffocating sense of guilt.

He was a ghost in this machine, a shadow in the starlight. But the starlight was becoming too bright, too real, and he was a man who had forgotten how to live in the light. He had a mission, a duty to his country, but he also had a heart, a heart that was pounding a frantic rhythm against his ribs, a heart that was getting dangerously close to falling in love with the very man he was supposed to betray.

The final piece of the puzzle was in his hand, a small, innocuous USB drive, a tiny vessel of truth in a sea of lies. He held it in his hand, his thumb tracing the smooth plastic, his mind a whirlwind of conflicting emotions. He was a professional, a highly decorated agent with a pristine record. But he was also a man who had found a home in the scent of rain and sandalwood, a man who had found a partner in this silent, dangerous dance.

He looked across the room, his eyes meeting Rhys's. Rhys was smiling, a small, shy smile that reached his eyes. He was a man who saw the world in numbers and patterns, a man who was oblivious to the vast, dark undercurrents of the world. He was a man who saw Finn not as a ghost, but as a partner, a friend, a person.

The USB drive felt heavy in his hand, a lead weight, a bomb waiting to go off. He had to make a choice. His duty to his country, his duty to his mission, or his heart. The choice was not as simple as it seemed. It was a choice between two different kinds of loyalty, two different kinds of love.

He stood, his movements slow and deliberate. He walked across the room, the distance between them feeling like a chasm, a vast, empty space that separated their two separate worlds. He stopped in front of Rhys's desk, the USB drive hidden in his hand.

"I need to talk to you," he said, his voice a low, raw whisper.

Rhys looked up, his smile fading, his eyes, so liquid and deep, filled with a sudden, sharp clarity. He saw the tension in Finn's shoulders, the raw, unfiltered emotion in his eyes. He saw the truth, a truth Finn had tried so hard to hide.

"What is this?" he asked, his voice a strangled gasp. "What have you done?"

Finn's heart hammered a frantic, furious rhythm against his ribs. He had betrayed him. He had chosen him, and in doing so, he had betrayed him. He was a man caught between two worlds, a ghost in the machine, a shadow in the starlight. He was a man who had found a home, and in doing so, had destroyed it.

He pulled back, his heart pounding a frantic rhythm against his ribs, a flicker of something he can't afford to feel.

Chapter 2

A Dangerous Proximity

The air in the executive office was a thick, stagnant fog of tension. The scent of polished mahogany and stale coffee hung heavy, a bitter, metallic tang from the recent storm's ozone adding to the suffocating atmosphere. Finn sat with his back ramrod straight, a posture of forced discipline that belied the roaring storm in his gut. The cold veneer of "Shadow" was a second skin he couldn't afford to shed, not with Dimitri Petrov sitting across from him. The patriarch's silver-streaked hair caught the glint of the massive chandelier above, his pale, glacial eyes sweeping over the financial ledgers with a predatory stillness. The silence in the room was a palpable thing, a coiled serpent ready to strike.

Dimitri's fingers, adorned with a single, heavy signet ring, tapped a rhythmic pattern on the page—each tap a hammer blow against Finn's meticulously constructed composure. The sound was an aural manifestation of Finn's mounting panic. "These figures, Kage," Dimitri's voice was a low growl, an engine idling just before a race. "The quarterly revenue from the Eastside docks. They seem… optimistic."

Finn's blood ran cold. The numbers were deliberately falsified, a minor, almost imperceptible inflation he had engineered to cover the slow, steady bleed of information he was siphoning from the family's illegal operations. He had spent weeks on this, weaving a tapestry of plausible lies so intricate it should have been invisible. But Dimitri, with a single icy glare, was threatening to unravel it all. Finn's jaw tightened, a muscle jumping in his cheek. His gaze was fixed on the page, not daring to look up and let the man see the flicker of panic in his eyes. He felt the cold sweat on the back of his neck, the primal urge to fight, to run, to tear down this facade and expose the truth.

"They are accurate, sir," Finn said, his voice a flat monotone. The words were a practiced lie, a performance he had rehearsed a thousand times. He had contingency plans for every possible scenario, every question, every accusation. But Dimitri's cold, calculating gaze was not a scenario; it was a reality, a direct threat.

Dimitri's lips, a thin, cruel line, curved into a mirthless smile. He looked up, his eyes meeting Finn's, and for a fleeting, terrifying moment, Finn felt utterly seen. His heart hammered against his ribs, a frantic, desperate drumbeat. "Are they, Kage? Because my chief accountant seems to think otherwise."

This was it. His years of work, the lies, the suppressed instincts—all of it would come crashing down in a single, catastrophic moment. Dimitri's eyes were narrowed, his attention a laser beam of suspicion. He gestured to a subordinate, a hulking alpha with a face like a storm cloud. "Get Rhys. I want him to look at these figures. I want him to tell me if they are, in fact, accurate."

The subordinate, a man named Grigor, nodded and lumbered toward the door, his movements heavy and menacing. Finn's mind was a whirlwind of panic. Rhys. The quiet, unassuming omega with the soft eyes and the scent of rain and sandalwood. The man who was his Achilles' heel, his greatest weakness. Rhys would see the lie. Rhys would see the ghost numbers, the forged entries, the false trail that led to nothing. He would expose Finn, and Finn's mission, his life, would be over.

But before Grigor could reach him, Rhys's voice, quiet but clear, cut through the suffocating silence. It was a lifeline, a beacon in the darkness.

"With respect, sir," Rhys said, his head still bowed over his own ledger, his fingers a blur of motion. "There's no need. The discrepancy is not in the quarterly revenue, but in the monthly expenditure for security personnel. The numbers are off by a fraction of a percentage, a rounding error. I can fix it."

Dimitri's gaze snapped to Rhys, his eyes narrowing. "You've already looked at these?" he asked, the words a low, dangerous growl.

Rhys looked up, his gaze meeting Dimitri's with quiet, unwavering confidence. "No, sir. Not these. But I know these numbers. I live these numbers. They are in my head." He gestured to the ledger in front of Finn. "The figures he has are accurate. The error is in the security expenditure. A misplaced decimal point. It's an easy mistake to make."

Finn's mind, a whirlwind of panic a moment ago, now snapped into focus. Rhys, with his photographic memory and innate understanding of the family's finances, had just created a perfect, plausible lie. He had corrected Finn's mistake, not by pointing it out, but by inventing a new, more plausible one. A ghost number. A lie tucked away in plain sight. It was a masterpiece of deceit, a brilliant, subtle act of defiance that left Finn breathless.

Dimitri stared at Rhys, his eyes a cold, hard thing, a predator sizing up his prey. He saw an unassuming omega, a quiet numbers man. He saw weakness. And he saw nothing else. He gestured to Finn with a curt nod. "Fix it."

"Yes, sir," Finn said, his voice a monotone, his face a carefully constructed mask of disinterest. He gave a small, formal nod to Dimitri, and then, without a word, he walked out of the office, the click of the door closing behind him a final, heavy punctuation. He didn't look back, but he could feel the weight of Rhys's gaze on his back, a silent plea hanging in the air like a ghost of its own.

As he walked down the empty hallway, the low murmur of Dimitri's voice echoing behind the closed door, Finn's heart pounded a frantic, furious rhythm against his ribs. He felt a cold dread settle in his stomach, a feeling he hadn't experienced since his first mission. He had left Rhys alone with the monster, and the thought was a knife twisting in his gut.

He stopped at the end of the hallway, a dark corner where the shadows were thick and deep. He leaned against the cool wall, his eyes closed, his breathing coming in ragged gasps. He could still smell the rain and sandalwood, a ghost scent that clung to his clothes, a constant reminder of the fragile, dangerous connection that was forming between them. A connection he couldn't afford. A connection that was getting dangerously close to becoming something real, something he was supposed to destroy.

He pulled out his phone, his fingers hovering over a contact he hadn't used in months. He was violating protocol, breaking a rule he had sworn to uphold. But the thought of Rhys, of his scent, of the small, hopeful smile he had given him, was a more powerful force than any rule. He typed out a message, his fingers clumsy and slow, the words a raw, unfiltered cry from his heart.

"Are you okay?"

He stared at the screen, the blue light illuminating his face in the dark of the car. He wasn't sure why he was doing this, why he was risking everything for a man he was supposed to be a ghost to. But he couldn't stop. He had to know. He had to hear his voice, or at least see a sign that he was safe. The silence stretched, a long, agonizing moment of waiting. He held his breath, his heart pounding a frantic rhythm against his ribs. And then, the phone vibrated. A single word, a single, blessed word, appeared on the screen, a beacon of hope in the darkness.

"Yes."

Finn let out a long, shuddering breath, the tension in his shoulders melting away. He wasn't sure what he had expected, what he had feared. But the single word was enough. It was a lifeline, a connection, a small, fragile thread of hope in the vast, dangerous web he was caught in.

Later that night, the city lights blurred into a watercolor of shimmering gold and silver, a beautiful, chaotic painting of a world Finn was trying to destroy. He was a ghost in this machine, an anachronism in this world of polished wood and hushed tones. But now, there was a ghost of something else. A ghost of a smile, a ghost of a touch, a ghost of a scent that clung to his clothes and his skin. He was a ghost, but he was no longer alone. He had a partner in this silent, dangerous dance, a partner he was getting dangerously close to falling in love with.

He found himself in a quiet, secluded hallway, a place where the shadows were thick and deep. He had been waiting for Rhys for what felt like an eternity, the minutes stretching into hours. He had to talk to him. He had to understand.

A door at the end of the hallway opened, and Rhys emerged, his head bowed, his shoulders slumped. He moved with a quiet, weary grace, a man who carried the weight of the world on his shoulders. He didn't see Finn at first, his gaze fixed on the floor, his mind a million miles away.

"Rhys," Finn said, his voice a low, intense whisper.

Rhys's head snapped up, his eyes wide with surprise. He saw Finn, a tall, muscular alpha standing in the shadows, his face a mask of unreadable intensity. He saw the cold, gray eyes that seemed to see right through him, the sharp jawline, the powerful shoulders. He saw "Shadow," the quiet, unassuming numbers man. But tonight, he saw something else. He saw a man, raw and unfiltered, his defenses down, his guard a broken thing.

"Finn," Rhys said, his voice a soft, breathless murmur.

Finn stepped out of the shadows, his presence a sudden, sharp intake of air in the quiet hallway. He stopped in front of Rhys, his gaze fixed on his face, a raw, unfiltered thing. He reached out, his hand hovering in the air between them, a silent question.

"Thank you," Finn said, the words a low, raw whisper. "You saved me. You saved everything."

Rhys flinched, his eyes wide. He looked away, his gaze falling to the floor. "I didn't do anything," he said, his voice a soft, breathless murmur. "I just... the numbers were wrong. I just fixed them."

"You didn't just fix them," Finn said, his voice intense. "You created a new lie to cover my lie. You protected me. You protected the entire operation."

Rhys looked up, his eyes meeting Finn's. A small, shy smile touched his lips, a ghost of a smile that reached his eyes. "I just… I felt I had to. I don't know why."

"I do," Finn said, his voice a low, intense whisper. "You're a good man, Rhys. A good omega."

Rhys flinched, his eyes wide with surprise. He looked away, his gaze falling to the floor. "I'm a ghost, Finn. A quiet omega. I'm a ghost in this machine, just like you."

Finn's gut twisted with guilt and an unwanted protectiveness toward Rhys. He was grateful, but terrified of what this secret alliance could mean for both of them. He had made a choice, and in doing so, he had sealed their fate. He had chosen him, and in doing so, he had betrayed him. He was a man caught between two worlds, a ghost in the machine, a shadow in the starlight. He was a man who had found a home, and in doing so, had destroyed it.

Chapter 3

The Broken Mask

The cold, sterile air of Finn's apartment felt like a tomb. The city lights, a distant, shimmering blur through the floor-to-ceiling windows, offered no warmth, no comfort. Finn sat on the edge of his bed, his knuckles white against the cool, rough texture of the comforter. His body was a cage, and the animal inside was beginning to stir.

The first tremors of a long-suppressed heat cycle had begun, a simmering fire beneath his cold exterior. He had been suppressing his biology for years, a necessary evil for a man living a lie. But now, with his mission at a crucial point, with the constant, overwhelming presence of Rhys, the quiet, unassuming omega with the scent of rain and sandalwood, his body was fighting back.

A low growl rumbled in his chest, a primal, guttural sound that was foreign to his ears. He had spent years perfecting the art of being "Shadow," the quiet, unassuming numbers man. But the mask was cracking, and the alpha underneath was fighting to get out. The physical and emotional need was consuming, a tidal wave of raw, unfiltered desire that threatened to drown him.

He stood, his movements a blur of uncontrolled energy. He paced the length of his apartment, his powerful alpha frame a caged animal, his mind a whirlwind of conflicting emotions. He was a man of protocol, a man of discipline, a man of rules. And the first rule of his mission was simple: do not get attached.

Do not get close. Do not form a personal connection. He had broken all three.

Desperate, he grabbed his keys and a jacket, the cold night air a welcome assault against his heated skin. He needed to clear his head. He needed to get away from the suffocating silence of his apartment, from the phantom scent of rain and sandalwood that clung to him like a ghost.

The streets of Chicago were a symphony of sirens and distant thunder, a beautiful, chaotic painting of a world Finn was trying to destroy. He drove, his movements a blur of uncontrolled energy, his mind a whirlwind of conflicting emotions. He was a man with no destination, a ghost haunting a city that had no place for him. He was a man who had forgotten how to live in the light, a man who was getting dangerously close to falling in love with the very man he was supposed to betray.

He found himself in a quiet, secluded neighborhood, a place of small, independent cafes and bookstores. He saw a small cafe, a single light burning in the window, a beacon in the darkness. He pulled over, his car a dark shadow against the rain-slicked street. He didn't know why he was there, what he was looking for. But he knew he couldn't go home, not yet.

He sat in his car, his head resting against the cool glass, his eyes closed. He was a man of protocol, a man of discipline, a man of rules. And the first rule of his mission was simple: do not get attached. Do not get close. Do not form a personal connection. He had broken all three.

Suddenly, a figure emerged from the cafe, a small, solitary figure that moved with a quiet, weary grace. It was Rhys. He was a ghost in the night, a man who carried the weight of the world on his shoulders. He looked troubled and alone, his head bowed, his shoulders slumped.

Rhys, sensing Finn's distress, approached him. There's an uncharacteristic vulnerability in Finn's posture that draws him in. Rhys invites him to sit, offering him a warm tea. He saw the cold, gray eyes that seemed to see right through him, the sharp jawline, the powerful shoulders. He saw "Shadow," the quiet, unassuming numbers man. But tonight, he saw something else. He saw a man, raw and unfiltered, his defenses down, his guard a broken thing.

"Finn," Rhys said, his voice a soft, breathless murmur.

Finn's head snapped up, his eyes wide with surprise. He saw Rhys, a small, solitary figure standing in the rain, a beacon in the darkness. He saw the soft, liquid brown eyes, the gentle curve of his neck, the fine lines of his jaw. He saw the man who had become his Achilles' heel, his greatest weakness.

"Rhys," Finn said, his voice a low, raw whisper.

Rhys walked to the passenger side of the car, his hand hovering over the door handle. "Are you okay?" he asked, his voice soft, a soothing counterpoint to the storm raging inside Finn. "You look... troubled."

Finn shook his head, a gesture of dismissal. "I'm fine. Just... couldn't sleep."

"Me neither," Rhys said, a small, sad smile touching his lips. "It's a lot, isn't it? The numbers. The lies. The ghosts."

Finn's heart hammered a frantic, furious rhythm against his ribs. He had betrayed him. He had chosen him, and in doing so, he had betrayed him. He was a man caught between two worlds, a ghost in the machine, a shadow in the starlight. He was a man who had found a home, and in doing so, had destroyed it.

"Yeah," Finn said, his voice a low, raw whisper. "It's a lot."

Rhys opened the car door, the scent of rain and sandalwood filling the confined space. "Come inside," he said, his voice soft, a gentle invitation. "The tea is warm. And... you don't have to be a ghost with me."

Finn's heart hammered a frantic, furious rhythm against his ribs. He had made a choice, and in doing so, he had sealed their fate. He had chosen him, and in doing so, he had betrayed him. He was a man caught between two worlds, a ghost in the machine, a shadow in the starlight. He was a man who had found a home, and in doing so, had destroyed it.

He got out of the car, his movements slow and deliberate. He followed Rhys into the cafe, the warmth and the scent of brewing tea a welcome assault against his heated skin. They sat in a secluded booth in the back, the low hum of the coffee maker and the soft murmur of distant traffic the only sounds.

They talked for hours, sharing their fears and loneliness. The conversation deepened, and the emotional walls Finn had built began to crumble. He found himself sharing intimate truths about his past, his desires for a life he couldn't have. He was a man of protocol, a man of discipline, a man of rules. And the first rule of his mission was simple: do not get attached. Do not get close. Do not form a personal connection. He had broken all three.

Rhys listened, his eyes, so liquid and deep, fixed on Finn's face. He saw the raw, unfiltered emotion in his eyes, the uncharacteristic vulnerability in his posture. He saw a man, a shadow, a ghost in the machine. But tonight, he saw something else. He saw a man, raw and unfiltered, his defenses down, his guard a broken thing.

"I know," Rhys said, his voice a whisper, a ghost of a sound in the quiet cafe. "I'm a ghost, too. A quiet omega. I'm a ghost in this machine, just like you."

Finn's heart hammered a frantic, furious rhythm against his ribs. He had betrayed him. He had chosen him, and in doing so, he had betrayed him. He was a man caught between two worlds, a ghost in the machine, a shadow in the starlight. He was a man who had found a home, and in doing so, had destroyed it.

He reached across the table, his hand covering Rhys's, his touch a gentle, hesitant thing. "You're not a ghost, Rhys," he said, his voice a low, raw whisper. "You're the starlight. You're the one thing that shines in all this darkness."

Rhys's eyes widened, his gaze sweeping over the numbers, the lies, the vast, dark tapestry of deceit. He looked up, his eyes meeting Finn's, a look of shock, of betrayal, of pure, unadulterated fear. "What are you talking about?" he asked, his voice a strangled gasp. "What have you done?"

Finn's heat, a long-suppressed fire, flared to life, a searing, all-consuming heat that threatened to consume him. He was a man of protocol, a man of discipline, a man of rules. And the first rule of his mission was simple: do not get attached. Do not get close. Do not form a personal connection. He had broken all three.

He stood, his movements slow and deliberate. He pulled Rhys to his feet, his gaze fixed on his face, his eyes a raw, unfiltered thing. He had made a choice, and in doing so, he had sealed their fate. He had chosen him, and in doing so, he had betrayed him. He was a man caught between two worlds, a ghost in the machine, a shadow in the starlight. He was a man who had found a home, and in doing so, had destroyed it.

Chapter 4

The Unforeseen Consequence

The heat cycle, a demon Finn had kept caged for so long with a cocktail of suppressants and sheer, brute willpower, erupted not with a slow, simmering fever, but in a violent, uncontrollable blaze. It was as if a dam had burst inside him, and the torrent of raw, primal need ripped the last vestiges of "Shadow" from his mind. The carefully constructed mental walls that had taken a decade to build—walls of discipline, of cold detachment, of controlled instinct—crumbled into dust. He was no longer a man; he was a vessel of pure, desperate hunger.

In the small, quiet cafe, the world shrank to a maelstrom of sensory overload. Every detail was magnified, every sound an assault, every scent a weapon. The smell of coffee, so comforting moments before, became a sharp, acrid assault on his senses, a bitter, metallic tang that burned in his nostrils. The low hum of the refrigerator was no longer background noise; it was a deafening roar that vibrated through his bones, a constant, irritating thrumming that frayed his already-shredded nerves. The flickering fluorescent lights above the counter pulsed with an unbearable intensity, casting stark shadows that danced and twisted in his peripheral vision.

And then there was the scent. The scent of rain and sandalwood, Rhys's scent, was no longer a ghost but a physical presence, a thick, intoxicating cloud that clung to the air and settled deep in his lungs. It was a siren's call, a promise of salvation in a sea of pure, agonizing need. It was a scent that spoke of safety, of comfort, of home—a concept Finn hadn't allowed himself to entertain in years. It was a scent that cut through the fog of his burgeoning heat, a beacon that pulled him toward it with an irresistible, gravitational force.

Finn's meticulously constructed world shattered in that instant. His body, once a finely tuned weapon, was now a vessel of pure, desperate hunger. The first sign was a deep, involuntary growl that vibrated up from his chest, a sound so raw and animalistic it shocked him even in his compromised state. His hands, which had been clenched on the edge of the table, trembled with a violent intensity. He stumbled out of the booth, his powerful legs feeling like lead, knocking over his half-empty cup of tea. The clatter of ceramic on tile echoed in his ears like a gunshot, but it was just a minor noise in the cacophony of his mind. Every nerve ending was screaming, every muscle in his powerful alpha body ached with a deep, consuming tension. He was no longer the calculated agent, the ghost in the machine; he was an alpha in distress, vulnerable and exposed. He felt his pupils dilate, his vision narrowing to a tunnel, focused only on the source of the intoxicating scent. He was an animal, all instinct, all need. The constant battle he had fought against his own nature was over, and instinct had won a brutal, undeniable victory.

Rhys was right behind him, his soft, concerned voice a lifeline in the chaos. "Finn? What's wrong? You're burning up." Rhys's words cut through the noise, a clear bell in the storm. He saw the alpha's distress not with fear, but with a deep-seated connection to the man he had come to admire. The scent of rain and sandalwood, so gentle and calming, was now a siren's call, a promise of relief. He watched as Finn, a man of such control and precision, came apart at the seams. It wasn't a facade, but a genuine, terrified unraveling.

Rhys, acting on instinct, grabbed Finn's arm. He felt the intense, shocking heat radiating from the alpha's skin, saw the wild, lost look in his gray eyes. He didn't question, he didn't hesitate. He knew, with the deep, ingrained certainty of an omega, what this was. He knew what Finn needed, even if Finn himself was too far gone to ask. "Come on, my place is just around the corner. You can't be out here." His voice was a soothing balm, his grip surprisingly strong, a tether to reality. He led Finn away from the cafe, away from the flickering streetlights and the distant hum of traffic, toward the quiet solitude of his own, more secluded apartment.

The journey was a blur for Finn, a series of disjointed flashes and sensations. He was a passenger in his own body, a captive of a primal storm. He was aware of the cold rain on his face, the slick pavement under his feet, and the steady, warm presence of Rhys's hand on his arm, a tether to reality. He stumbled, his powerful legs feeling like lead, but Rhys held him, his grip surprisingly strong. He was a pillar of calm in the midst of Finn's tempest, a beacon in the storm. The scent of him, that beautiful, intoxicating scent of rain and sandalwood, grew stronger with every step, and Finn's growls became a low, desperate moan. He needed it. He needed him. The world was nothing but the heat and the scent, a cruel dichotomy that promised both agony and bliss.

The apartment was a sanctuary. The moment the door closed behind them, the world outside ceased to exist. Inside, the world shrank to the two of them. The scent of Rhys's home—of books and fresh laundry and, most potently, his own subtle omega scent—was a potent mix that sent Finn's senses into overdrive. The raw, sensual energy between them became an undeniable, suffocating force. Finn's growls were more frequent now, his body trembling with the intensity of the heat. He was a ship caught in a storm, and Rhys was the only shore.

Rhys, in an act of profound compassion, helped Finn through the heat. He didn't shrink away from the alpha's raw need. He met it with a quiet strength, with a deep, unwavering empathy. He led him to the bedroom, the room filled with the soft scent of rain and sandalwood, and helped him lie down. Their bodies and souls entwined in a desperate intimacy, a whirlwind of intense emotions and physical sensation.

Finn's mind, clouded by the heat, found a brief moment of clarity. He looked at Rhys, at the gentle lines of his face, the soft, liquid brown eyes, the quiet strength in his touch. He saw not the ghost, but the man—the kind, quiet, brilliant omega who had saved him, not once, but twice. He was no longer a number in a ledger, no longer a ghost in the machine. He was Rhys. His Rhys. And in that moment, in the throes of a primal, uncontrollable need, Finn's heart, a frozen thing for so long, thawed.

Finn's heat subsiding, leaving him exhausted, emotionally raw, and with the terrifying realization of what he has done. He lies in Rhys's bed, the scent of rain and sandalwood heavy in the air, his body a map of bruised passion, his mind a whirlwind of guilt and dread. He was a man of protocol, a man of discipline, a man of rules. And the first rule of his mission was simple: do not get attached. Do not get close. Do not form a personal connection. He had broken all three, and in doing so, he had sealed their fate.

Chapter 5

The Confession

The world outside was a cold, indifferent gray. Rain, a soft, persistent drizzle, traced silver streaks down the windowpane, blurring the outline of the city's concrete towers. The sound was a quiet, hypnotic rhythm—a stark counterpoint to the roaring chaos that had defined the night before. Inside, the air was heavy and warm, a thick, humid stillness that hung in the space between the waking world and the one Finn was just leaving.

He came to consciousness slowly, a gradual return to a body that felt both impossibly weary and humming with a strange, latent energy. The sheets were a tangled mess of silk and cotton, twisted around his powerful legs. The mattress, softer than the stark, clinical slab he was accustomed to, cradled his body in a way that felt both foreign and profoundly right. He lay there for a moment, his eyes still closed, letting the details of the room seep into his senses. The scent was the first thing—a heady, complex fragrance that was a remnant of their desperate intimacy. It was a potent blend of their two scents, a new, third entity born of their heat. The rain and sandalwood of Rhys, now laced with the metallic, sharp tang of a possessive alpha's scent. It was a brand, a claim, a physical manifestation of a bond he had never intended to forge.

A low, guttural growl, a lingering echo of the alpha he had been, rumbled in his chest. A deep, instinctual part of him, the part he had spent a decade burying, screamed with a triumphant, possessive satisfaction. But the conscious, rational part of his mind, the part that was Agent Finn Kage, was a cold, hard knot of dread. He cracked open his eyes.

He was alone.

The space beside him was a mess of rumpled sheets, but it was empty. The sudden absence was a punch to the gut. The low light of the Chicago dawn, filtered through the city's perpetual haze, cast a pale, weak glow across the bedroom. It illuminated the quiet details: a small stack of worn paperbacks on a nightstand, a half-empty glass of water, the faint outline of a framed photograph on the dresser. The room was not sterile like his own safe house, but lived-in, soft, and warm. And in that soft, warm light, the hard, cold truth began to crystallize.

He pushed himself up, the muscles in his torso protesting with a dull ache. He was completely bare, his skin a canvas of hickeys and fading love bites. The evidence of his complete and total surrender. His alpha was sated, but the man was terrified. He swung his legs over the side of the bed, his feet finding the cool, smooth wood of the floorboards. A sharp, metallic tang in the air caught his attention, a scent that was a new and unwelcome note in the symphony of the room. It was the scent of fear, but not his own. It was Rhys.

His eyes darted around the room, searching, his trained instincts kicking in. Where was he? A quick scan of the bedroom and the attached bathroom revealed nothing. He moved toward the open doorway, his senses on high alert. The scent was stronger now, a thin, wavering thread of fear mixed with something else. Something he couldn't quite place. He found him in the living room, a small, solitary figure standing with his back to the window, the gray light framing his delicate silhouette.

Rhys was a portrait of trembling vulnerability. He was dressed in a pair of Finn's sweatpants, the soft gray fabric a stark contrast to his pale skin. They were too long, their hem dragging on the floor, and the waistband was cinched with a taut pull. He held a small, white object in his hands, his fingers wrapped around it so tightly his knuckles were bloodless. His shoulders were hunched, a defensive posture that spoke of a deep, primal fear.

Finn's heart hammered against his ribs, a frantic, furious rhythm. He took a single, slow step into the room, his voice a low, hesitant murmur. "Rhys?"

Rhys's head snapped up. His eyes, normally a soft, liquid brown, were wide, dark pools of unadulterated terror. He looked at Finn, at the tall, powerful alpha standing half-naked in the doorway, and the terror intensified, a new kind of fear that Finn recognized instantly. It wasn't the fear of an omega for a powerful alpha; it was the fear of an omega for a powerful alpha who was also a stranger.

Rhys's trembling hands, in a jerky, uncontrolled motion, held up the small, white object. The movement was a slow-motion nightmare for Finn. He saw it. A plastic stick. Two distinct, parallel lines of vivid pink. A positive pregnancy test.

The world seemed to spin on its axis, a violent, sickening lurch that took the air from his lungs. The reality of what had happened, the full and terrifying weight of it, crashed down on him with the force of a tidal wave. This wasn't just a moment of weakness. It wasn't just a compromised mission. This was a consequence. This was a life. This was his, their, child.

Rhys's lips, a pale, trembling line, parted. The words that came out were a soft, breathless gasp, a fragile sound that shattered the silence. "I… I don't know how…"

His mind, a fortress of logic and protocol, was now a battlefield. The training, the years of discipline, the cold, hard logic of his mission screamed at him to run, to create a new lie, to disappear. But the alpha, the possessive, primal part of him, roared with a deafening certainty: Ours. Mine. Family. Protect.

He moved forward, a slow, deliberate step, his eyes never leaving Rhys's face. He stopped a few feet away, a chasm of fear and unspoken words between them. He had to tell him. He had to pull back the curtain and expose the monster he was. He was an agent, a ghost, a liar. He had to confess.

"Rhys," he said, his voice a low, raw whisper that felt foreign in his own ears. "Rhys, I have to tell you something. I..."

Rhys took a step back, his shoulders hitting the cool glass of the windowpane with a soft thud. He hugged himself, his body shaking uncontrollably. "Who are you?" he asked, the words a desperate, trembling plea. "You're not Shadow. You're not the numbers man. Who are you?"

Finn closed his eyes, a brief, agonizing moment of surrender. He felt the cold, hard walls of his facade crumble, the mask he had worn for years peeling away like burnt skin. The man he had been was gone, replaced by a ghost of his true self.

"My name is Finn," he said, the words a heavy, physical weight on his tongue. "My name is Finn Kage. I'm an FBI agent."

The confession hung in the air, a final, definitive death sentence to the fragile, beautiful lie they had built. Rhys's eyes widened, the last vestiges of hope vanishing from them. He didn't scream. He didn't cry. He just stood there, a small, trembling omega, the full and terrible weight of Finn's words settling on his shoulders like a shroud.

"An agent?" Rhys whispered, the words a raw, broken thing. "You're... a federal agent?" He looked down at the pregnancy test in his hands, then back up at Finn. A slow, agonizing realization dawned on his face, the pieces of the puzzle clicking into place with a horrifying certainty. "You were... you were here to... to destroy us. To destroy my family."

Finn took another step forward, his hand outstretched, a silent plea for him to not pull away. "Rhys, listen to me. I..."

"Don't," Rhys said, his voice now a low, fierce thing, a broken whisper of a command. "Don't touch me. You're a lie. Everything was a lie. The cafe. The numbers. The... the heat." His gaze fell to Finn's naked body, and for a fleeting, agonizing moment, Finn saw a flash of disgust in his eyes. It was a rejection more profound than any blow.

Finn's heart, a frozen thing for so long, felt like it was being torn from his chest. "No. No, Rhys. That wasn't a lie. That was... that was real."

"Was it?" Rhys asked, a bitter, mirthless laugh escaping his lips. "Or was it just another part of the game? Did you just... use me? To get closer to Dimitri? To get the information you needed?"

The questions were a series of sharp, precise blows, each one landing on an open wound. Finn's jaw clenched, a muscle jumping in his cheek. He had to be honest. He had to tell him everything.

"I am an agent," Finn said, his voice a low, raw thing, a confession without any pretense. "My mission was to infiltrate Dimitri's inner circle. To find evidence of his money laundering, his arms deals, his human trafficking. My codename is Shadow. I've been in his organization for three years. Every number I've ever shown you was a fabrication. A ghost in the machine."

Rhys's body, which had been a statue of fear, now began to shake with a furious, uncontrolled intensity. "Three years?" he said, his voice rising, a sharp, broken sound. "Three years you've been here, pretending to be a loyal accountant? Pretending to be one of us? You've been watching me. You've been... observing me."

"I was," Finn said, the single word a testament to his own monstrous deceit. "At first, you were just a number. A data point. The omega accountant with an eidetic memory who was too valuable to be a problem. But then... then I got to know you. And I realized that you weren't a part of the machine. You were just a ghost, just like me."

"Don't you dare," Rhys said, his voice a low, furious hiss. "Don't you dare pretend you know me. You don't know me. You know my numbers. You know the details of my life that you've been recording for your report. You don't know me. You don't know the man who was lonely and desperate and just wanted... just wanted to be seen."

The words were a brutal, unfiltered truth that ripped Finn's composure to shreds. He saw it all then. The quiet smiles in the office. The late nights in the cafe. The soft, gentle touch that had been a silent plea for connection. All of it, a genuine, profound act of friendship from a lonely omega. And all of it, a lie from a professional ghost.

Rhys's eyes, a storm of tears he was fighting to hold back, looked down at the pregnancy test in his hands. A new wave of pure, unadulterated panic swept across his face. "And now... now this. You got what you wanted, didn't you? You got your evidence. You got your way into the heart of the family. All you needed was an omega, and you found one. A lonely, naive omega."

"No," Finn said, his voice a desperate, frantic thing. "Rhys, no. I swear to you. I never... the heat. I tried to stop it. I took the suppressants. I tried to lock it down. It was a mistake. A professional failing. But the bond... the bond is real. The heat was real. The feelings... they're real."

He took another step forward, his hand still outstretched, a silent, trembling offer of comfort. This time, Rhys didn't pull away. He just stood there, a small, trembling figure in the gray light, his face a mask of profound, devastating betrayal. He looked at Finn, at the powerful, naked alpha who had just confessed to being a spy, and a single tear, hot and silent, rolled down his cheek.

"I can't believe you," Rhys said, the words a soft, broken whisper. "I can't believe you were lying to me all this time."

"I know," Finn said, the words a raw, unfiltered admission of guilt. "I know. And I'm sorry. I'm so, so sorry." He took a final step, closing the distance between them. He reached out, his hand gently cupping Rhys's cheek, his touch a soft, hesitant thing. Rhys flinched, but he didn't pull away. He just stood there, a small, trembling statue of pain.

Finn's thumb, rough and calloused from a lifetime of combat, gently brushed away the tear. The action was a silent promise, a vow. He looked at Rhys, at the devastation etched on his face, and his mind, once a fortress of protocol, was now a burning furnace of a new, single purpose. He had failed his mission. He had compromised his life. He had broken every rule. But in doing so, he had found something more important than any mission. He had found a family. And he was going to protect them, no matter the cost.

"I swear to you, Rhys," Finn said, his voice a low, fierce whisper, a vow that was a physical weight in the air between them. "I swear to you on my life. I will protect you. I will protect this child. I will protect you from Dimitri, from the FBI, from everyone. I will do whatever it takes. I will dismantle this entire operation from the inside out, if I have to. I will walk away from my life. I will disappear with you. I will do whatever you want. Just... just don't look at me like that."

Rhys looked up, his eyes meeting Finn's. He saw the sharp, gray eyes of a predator, but they were now filled with a raw, unfiltered love. He saw the face of the man who had lied to him, but he also saw the face of the man who had just risked everything to tell him the truth. He saw the face of the man who had just given him a child. He saw the face of a man who was now just as lost, just as terrified, as he was.

His fear, a raw, primal thing, was now mixed with a new, strange emotion: a profound, aching love for this man. This liar. This spy. He was a monster, but he was his monster. He was a threat, but he was his protector. He was a lie, but he was a lie that had produced a beautiful, terrifying truth.

Rhys's body, which had been a statue of fear, now began to tremble with a new kind of intensity. He dropped the pregnancy test to the floor, the soft thud a final punctuation to their conversation. He reached up, his hand a small, fragile thing against Finn's cheek, his touch a silent question.

"I'm so scared," he whispered, the words a soft, broken plea. "He'll find out. Dimitri will find out. He'll... he'll kill us both."

Finn's arms, powerful and sure, wrapped around Rhys's body, pulling him into a possessive, crushing embrace. He held him close, his scent, now a soft, comforting blanket of rain and sandalwood, filling his senses. He held him like he was the only thing in the world that mattered. Because he was.

"He won't," Finn said, his voice a low, fierce whisper, a promise that was a physical weight. "I won't let him. I will die before I let him touch you. I will die before I let him touch our child."

And in that moment, huddled together in the gray light of a Chicago dawn, their shared secret heavier than a physical weight, they both knew that their lives, once separate and alone, were now a single, tangled knot of love, betrayal, and a terrible, beautiful truth. Their lives would never be the same. The ghosts had found each other, and in doing so, they had brought a new ghost into the world. A ghost that was a life. A ghost that was a child.

Chapter 6

A Fugitive's Alliance

The gray light of the dawn filtered through the rain-streaked window, illuminating a scene of quiet devastation. The air, which had been thick with the scent of their desperate intimacy, now held a new, colder fragrance: the sharp, metallic tang of fear and the subtle, burning afterimage of betrayal. Finn, still half-naked and a map of bruised passion, stood motionless, his powerful frame a stark, imposing shadow in the pale light. Across from him, Rhys was a statue carved from frozen grief, his face a perfect mask of profound, uncomprehending pain. The words "I'm an FBI agent" had not just shattered their fragile bond; they had cleaved the world in two.

A slow, agonizing silence stretched between them, a chasm of unspoken words and shattered trust. Finn's heart hammered a frantic, desperate rhythm against his ribs, a frantic drum against the silence. He watched Rhys, his gaze unwavering, searching for any sign of movement, any flicker of a response. But Rhys remained still, his hands still pressed to his stomach, a protective gesture that was both a shield and a quiet, agonizing reminder of the new life between them.

The moment seemed to last an eternity, a slow-motion descent into an abyss of his own making. Finn had expected rage. He had prepared himself for screams, for accusations, for a physical lashing out. But this silent, trembling paralysis was worse. It was the quiet of a world ending.

A tremor, almost imperceptible at first, ran through Rhys's body. His chin, which had been tucked into his chest, lifted slowly. His eyes, swollen but dry, met Finn's. There was no longer terror there. The pure, unadulterated fear had been burned away by a colder, harder fire. What Finn saw now was a terrible, beautiful thing: the flinty resolve of a man who has lost everything and has nothing left but a raw, fierce instinct for survival. The quiet omega was gone, replaced by a desperate, terrified survivor.

"The files," Rhys said, his voice a low, raspy sound that scraped against the silence. He wasn't asking. He was stating a fact. "You were here for the files. For the ledgers."

Finn swallowed hard, the muscles in his throat tight. He nodded once, a slow, deliberate movement. "That was the mission. The ledgers, the transactions, the money-laundering schemes. They're the key to taking Dimitri down."

A bitter, mirthless laugh, a sound like glass shattering, escaped Rhys's lips. "The key? I am the key."

He moved then, a jerky, deliberate motion that broke the spell. He walked past Finn, not touching him, not looking at him, but leaving a wake of cold air in his absence. He went to a small, oak writing desk tucked into a corner of the living room, a space Finn had never seen him use. He opened a drawer, pulled out a small, leather-bound notebook, and placed it on the polished wood.

"This," Rhys said, his voice now steadier, laced with a new, terrifying confidence. "This is the truth of the Petrov family. Every dirty deal. Every offshore account. Every single illegal transaction. I kept track of it all. In my head."

Finn's sharp, gray eyes narrowed, a cold, professional assessment kicking in despite his personal turmoil. "In your head? The Petrovs have millions of transactions every year. It's impossible to track them all."

Rhys looked at him then, a shadow of his old, quiet brilliance flashing in his eyes. "Not for me. I'm not just an accountant. I'm a Petrov. I have a photographic memory. Every number I've ever seen, every date, every account, every offshore transaction, it's all right here." He tapped the side of his head with a trembling finger. "Dimitri thinks he's a genius. He thinks his system of ghost companies and fake identities is airtight. But he's wrong. It's a web of numbers, and I'm the only spider who knows where every thread goes."

The revelation hit Finn with the force of a physical blow. He had been chasing ghosts, fabricating evidence, and building a case brick by brick, when the key to the entire operation was right there, living and breathing, a quiet omega with a mind like a steel trap. He had not just compromised his mission; he had stumbled into the heart of it.

A new kind of plan, a desperate, frantic, and terrifying new course of action, began to form in his mind. The old rules, the old protocols, the old mission were gone. They had been annihilated by the truth of this room, by the small, trembling omega with the terrifying gift, and by the new life growing inside him.

"You're a liability," Finn said, the words a raw, unfiltered expression of the conflict raging inside him. "You're too valuable to be a witness. You're too dangerous to be a ghost. You're a target. Dimitri will hunt you down and he'll kill you to keep his secrets buried."

Rhys met his gaze, the flinty resolve in his eyes hardening into a cold, unbreakable steel. "Then we don't let him. We run. We take his secrets with us, and we use them to bring his empire to its knees." He gestured to the leather-bound notebook. "This is a decoy. A little gift for Dimitri to find when he comes looking. It will buy us a few hours. But the real information..." He tapped his head again. "...is safe. It's with us. We'll be ghosts. The kind you can't catch."

The air crackled with a newfound tension, a dangerous, electric energy that was a stark contrast to the quiet devastation of moments before. The dynamic had shifted. It was no longer Finn, the hunter, and Rhys, the prey. They were an alliance. Two fugitives, bound by a lie and a terrible truth, with a shared goal: survival.

"What do you need?" Finn asked, his voice low and guttural. He was an agent again, his mind racing through tactical possibilities, escape routes, resources. But the purpose was different now. The mission was no longer to dismantle an empire; it was to protect a life.

Rhys moved to the kitchen, his steps still hesitant but gaining speed, the primal instinct of an omega protecting his den a new, fierce light in his eyes. He opened a cupboard, pulling out a small, duffel-style bag. He began to fill it with essentials. A toothbrush. A change of clothes. A small, nondescript wallet.

"We need cash. Dimitri keeps an emergency safe in his study. The combination is my brother's birthday. I memorized it when I was a child. The date is a lie, but the numbers are true. We also need passports. Fake ones. I know a guy. He's an associate of my father's. He has a small, quiet business on the outskirts of the city. He owes Dimitri, but he also owes me. I kept his secrets for him. He'll help us."

The plan was audacious. It was insane. It was brilliant. It was the only way. As Finn watched Rhys move with a new, frantic purpose, a sense of grim admiration filled him. The gentle, quiet omega was a viper. He had been living in the belly of the beast, collecting secrets, building a mental armory, just in case a day like this ever came. He wasn't a liability. He was a weapon.

Just as Finn's mind was racing to put a plan into motion, his cell phone, a burner phone he had been using to communicate with his handler, vibrated with a sharp, insistent buzz. The caller ID was a sequence of numbers he didn't recognize. He answered it, his voice a low, terse command. "Kage."

A frantic, breathless voice on the other end, a junior Petrov associate named Sergei, spoke in a rush of broken Russian. "Shadow. Get out. Get out now. Dimitri... he knows. He knows about the files. He knows about the pregnancy test. The one in the bathroom. The one you left behind. He knows."

The words were a physical blow, a cold, brutal shock that ripped the air from Finn's lungs. The pregnancy test. In the frantic chaos of the confession, the terror of the moment, he had forgotten about the test Rhys had dropped. A simple, white piece of plastic that had become a death sentence.

"Where is he?" Finn asked, his voice a low, dangerous growl.

"He's at the compound. He's tearing it apart. He's looking for the ledgers. He's looking for Rhys. He knows you're with him. Get out. He's sending men. He's sending everyone."

The line went dead.

Finn's heart, a frantic, furious drum, hammered a new, terrifying rhythm. He ran to the window, peering out into the still-drizzling street. He couldn't see anything. But he could hear it. In the distance, a sound like a low, angry swarm of bees. Cars. So many cars. They were coming.

"Rhys," Finn said, his voice a low, fierce command. "Now. We go now. They're coming."

Rhys, his face a mask of cold resolve, didn't flinch. He finished packing the last of the clothes into the duffel bag, his movements precise and quick. He handed Finn a small, nondescript bag. "Passports. They're fake, but they'll work. My contact's a genius."

Finn's jaw clenched. "Your contact is a ghost. He just made you a real one."

They raced to the back of the apartment, grabbing only what they needed. The duffel bag. The burner phones. A small, black satchel with Finn's spare handgun and a few clips of ammunition. He checked the clip on the gun, the familiar weight of the metal a small, comforting certainty in the roaring chaos. They were ready.

As they moved toward the back door, the silence of the building was shattered by the distant, furious wail of an alarm. Not just one. A hundred of them. A symphony of high-pitched, insistent screams that echoed down the halls and up the stairs. Dimitri had found the decoy. The game had begun.

They slipped out of the Petrov estate in the dead of night, leaving everything they'd ever known behind, just as the alarms began to wail.

Chapter 7

Hunted

The world had become a blur of gray asphalt and flickering neon signs. The stolen car, a nondescript Ford Taurus that had seen better days, rattled and groaned over the uneven Chicago pavement. The smell of stale cigarette smoke and cheap air freshener hung in the air, a nauseating mix that did little to calm the frantic, hammering rhythm of Finn's heart. He was behind the wheel, his knuckles white against the worn leather. Beside him, Rhys sat motionless, his gaze fixed on the blurred lights of the city. He was a small, quiet figure in the vast, roaring darkness, a beacon of calm in the storm.

They had been driving for an hour, a frantic, aimless flight from the wailing alarms of the Petrov compound. The sirens had faded into a distant memory, a faint echo on the wind. But the danger was real. It was a cold, physical presence that rode in the back seat, an invisible passenger that reminded them with every passing moment that they were on the run.

A small, flickering television screen in a grimy liquor store window caught Rhys's attention. He leaned forward, his face illuminated by the harsh, blue light of the screen. A grainy photograph flashed on the screen, a blurry, pixelated image of an alpha's face. Finn's face. The words beneath the photograph were a cold, brutal reality: "Rogue FBI Agent. Wanted for questioning in connection with Petrov family investigation. Bounty: undisclosed."

Rhys's hand, a small, trembling thing, reached out and gently touched Finn's arm. "Finn," he said, his voice a soft, low whisper.

Finn glanced at him, his gaze sharp and focused. "I know," he said, his voice a low, terse growl. "It's a cover-up. They'll brand me a rogue to protect their own. And to keep the investigation from going public. They'll want me back, but they won't want to admit I was one of them. The bounty is a distraction. They want me dead."

The full weight of the situation settled on Rhys's shoulders like a physical weight. The betrayal, the fear, the confusion... it all gave way to a new, terrible realization. Finn had not just betrayed his mission. He had burned every bridge. He was a rogue. A ghost with no home, no allies, and a price on his head. He had given up everything to protect Rhys, and now they were both hunted by two of the most powerful organizations in the city.

The burner phone in Finn's pocket buzzed with a sharp, insistent rhythm. The screen, a cold, sterile thing, showed a single, coded message from a former contact. The message was simple, but the meaning was clear.

"The Viper is hunting. The scent is fresh. Don't go to the nest. He will find you."

The Viper. Dimitri Petrov. The ruthless and paranoid head of the Petrov family. The man who had built his empire on a foundation of violence and manipulation. The man who was now hunting them down with a single, burning purpose: to kill them and bury their secret.

"What does it mean?" Rhys asked, his voice a small, fragile thing in the roaring silence of the car.

Finn's jaw clenched. "It means he knows we're on the run. It means he's sending his men. It means he's not going to stop until he finds us. And it means my old safe houses, my old contacts, my old life... they're all compromised." He turned the car down a small, deserted alley, the tires squealing in protest. The air was thick with the scent of damp concrete and rotting garbage. A rat, its eyes beady and bright, scurried into a dark corner.

A sudden, sharp movement in his rearview mirror caught Finn's attention. A black sedan. Not just any black sedan. A custom, bulletproofed Mercedes, the kind Dimitri's men drove. They were a hundred yards back, but they were gaining.

"Rhys," Finn said, his voice a low, fierce whisper. "Don't look back. Don't make a sound. Just hold on."

He slammed his foot down on the gas pedal, the engine roaring in protest. The car, a small, rattling thing, surged forward, its tires screaming against the asphalt. The black sedan behind them followed, a silent, menacing shadow in the rearview mirror. The chase was on.

They careened through the deserted streets of the industrial district, a frantic, high-speed ballet of death and survival. The scent of burning rubber and gasoline filled the air, a thick, nauseating perfume. Finn, his sharp, gray eyes focused and cold, wove the car through a maze of warehouses and shipping containers. He was a ghost again, but this time, he was a ghost on the run.

The black sedan, heavier and more powerful, was a relentless predator, gaining on them with every turn. They were closing the gap. Finn could see the glint of a rifle barrel in the back window. The adrenaline, a sharp, metallic taste in his mouth, was a familiar companion. But the fear, a cold, hard knot in his gut, was new. It wasn't his own fear. It was the fear for the small, trembling omega beside him.

"Hold on," Finn said, his voice a low, desperate growl. He veered the car sharply to the left, slamming the brakes. The car skidded on the wet pavement, the tires screaming in protest. They came to a sudden, jarring halt.

"Out," Finn commanded, his voice a low, sharp command. "Out now!"

He scrambled out of the car, grabbing the duffel bag and the satchel. Rhys followed, his movements slow and clumsy with a fear he was fighting to contain. The scent of his fear, a potent, coppery tang, filled the air. Finn grabbed him, his hand a steel vice around his arm, and pulled him into a dead run.

They ran. Through the darkness. Through a maze of shipping containers and forgotten crates. The sounds of shouting, of men on the hunt, echoed behind them. The black sedan, its engine roaring in protest, had slammed to a halt a few yards back. They were coming.

They ducked into a small, abandoned warehouse, the air thick with the smell of rust and dust. Finn pushed Rhys behind a stack of crates, his body a shield, his gun drawn. He held his breath, his senses on high alert. The sounds of men, their heavy boots thudding on the pavement, grew closer. The air was thick with the smell of their cologne, their cheap cigars, and their primal, possessive alpha scents.

The footsteps passed. The shouting faded into a distant murmur. They were gone. For now.

Finn let out a long, slow breath, the air a burning furnace in his lungs. He was soaked with sweat, his body trembling with the aftershocks of the chase. He looked at Rhys, at the small, quiet omega huddled behind the crates, his face a mask of profound, devastating terror. The reality of their situation, a cruel, brutal truth, settled on them both. They were fugitives. They were hunted. They were alone.

Finn's hand, a rough, calloused thing, reached out and gently touched Rhys's cheek. "It's okay," he said, his voice a low, raw whisper, a desperate promise. "We're safe. I won't let them touch you. I won't let them touch our child."

He led Rhys deeper into the warehouse, past the crates and the forgotten machinery. He found a small, hidden room, a space he had prepared a year ago for a mission that had gone sideways. It was a secret safe house. A place he had been saving for the worst-case scenario.

The room was small and nondescript, with a single bed and a small, rusted metal table. A few cans of food sat on a shelf, and a small, a single battery-powered lantern sat in the middle of the room. It was not a home. It was a bunker.

Finn helped Rhys onto the small, cot-like bed. He sat beside him, his arm a strong, comforting weight around his shoulders. He pulled him close, their bodies a single, shivering knot in the cold, desolate space.

The cold reality of their situation settled in, a final, definitive truth. They were fugitives, hunted by two powerful organizations. They were alone, with nothing but their wits and the deep, terrifying bond they had forged in the fire of their heat. The world they had known was gone, replaced by a new, dangerous existence, a life on a fragile thread. But as Finn held Rhys close, as he felt the small, trembling body in his arms, he knew one thing with a piercing, absolute certainty: he was not a ghost anymore. He was a father. He was a protector. He was a home. And for the first time in his life, he was not alone. The hunt had begun, but they were in it together.

Chapter 8

A Glimpse of Normalcy

The safe house was a cage forged of concrete and silence. Its existence was a testament to meticulous planning and a cold-blooded assessment of every conceivable danger. Finn had built it a year ago, an isolated steel bunker tucked within the belly of an abandoned warehouse in the industrial district of Chicago. The air, heavy with the scent of ozone, stale drywall, and the metallic tang of rust, was the antithesis of a home. There was no warmth here, no lingering aroma of coffee or old books, only the sterile, unforgiving presence of absolute security. A single, bare bulb hung from a frayed wire in the center of the room, casting a stark, uncompromising light that left no corner unexposed. The walls, painted a flat, clinical white, were scuffed and chipped, a map of forgotten failures and near-disasters.

The only piece of furniture in the room was a small, cot-like bed—a slab of worn canvas stretched over a steel frame—and a single, rusted metal table where the sputtering lantern now rested. A small cooler sat in the corner, its white plastic a beacon in the gloom, holding a meager ration of bottled water and canned food. The space was designed for survival, not for living, its every detail a reminder of the life they had been forced to abandon. And yet, for the first time in what felt like a lifetime, the air between Finn and Rhys was not thick with the acrid scent of fear. The low, guttural roar of their escape, the frantic drumming of their hearts in the abandoned warehouse, had receded into a distant, buzzing memory. The constant, gnawing threat of Dimitri's men and the FBI's agents had been momentarily pushed back, replaced by the suffocating quiet of their newfound reality.

Finn, ever the protector, moved through the space with the silent, predatory grace of a man who had spent his life in the shadows. He had a can opener in his hand, its steel teeth biting into a can of bland, unseasoned soup. The scrape and turn of the gears was the only sound in the room, a rhythmic, mechanical counterpoint to the quiet stillness of their shared grief. He set the open can on the metal table, along with a bottle of water, a silent offering of a peace he could not yet truly feel.

He watched Rhys from the corner of his eye. The omega was a small, delicate figure on the unforgiving cot, wrapped in one of Finn's too-large, too-warm t-shirts. The fabric, still carrying the faint, reassuring scent of his alpha nature, was a comfort in the sterile air.

Rhys's eyes were not wide with terror anymore. They were clouded with a deep, silent contemplation, a quiet processing of the monumental, life-altering events of the last twenty-four hours. He was a man who had lost everything—his home, his family, his life—and yet, there was a strange, terrifying strength in the way he held himself. The trembling, terrified omega of the morning was gone, replaced by a quiet, determined survivor. Finn had been trained to see weakness, to exploit it, to use it to his advantage. But in Rhys, he saw a resilience that was both astonishing and humbling. This omega was not fragile. He was a force. A quiet, formidable one.

Finn sat down on the floor, his back against the cool concrete wall, the hard surface a familiar comfort. He watched Rhys, allowing the silence to stretch between them, a fragile, unspoken truce.

"I was an accountant," Rhys said, his voice a low, raspy whisper that broke the silence. He was not speaking to Finn, but to the chipped paint on the wall. "My whole life, numbers. That was my world. Every ledger, every transaction, every dirty little secret. It was a language I understood. It was safe. It was predictable."

Finn's hand, a rough, calloused thing, rested on his knee. He remained silent, allowing Rhys to speak, allowing the words to fill the vast emptiness of the room. He knew, instinctively, that this was not a moment for strategy or for lies. This was a moment for truth.

"And now," Rhys continued, his voice barely a breath. "Now I'm a ghost. A fugitive. My life is a number on a wanted poster. And the man who made me a ghost… is an FBI agent." He turned his head slowly, his eyes meeting Finn's. There was no accusation in his gaze, no bitter rage. Only a deep, profound sadness.

"I am sorry," Finn said, the words a raw, honest confession. "I am so sorry, Rhys."

Rhys offered a small, sad smile, a fleeting, heartbreaking flash of emotion. "Sorry for what? For getting caught in the crossfire? For saving my life? For... for this?" His gaze fell to his stomach, a small, involuntary gesture of protection.

"For lying to you," Finn said, his voice a low, fierce murmur. "For making you a part of my mission. For making you a target. For all of it. I should have... I should have known better."

Rhys shook his head, a single, decisive movement. "You didn't know. You didn't know you were going to fall into my life. You didn't know you were going to get me pregnant. We didn't know. This... this is a consequence. Not a conspiracy."

The words, a gentle, understanding absolution, were a powerful, emotional blow. Finn had been prepared for a storm of anger, for a flood of accusations, but this quiet, heartbreaking acceptance was something he had never considered. It was a testament to the man he had been, and the man he had become. And in that moment, in that cold, sterile room, Finn realized that Rhys's strength was not in his ability to fight, but in his ability to forgive.

The silence returned, a fragile, tender thing. It was broken by a sudden, jarring sound from the small, portable radio that sat on the metal table. The static cleared, and a slow, bluesy melody, a quiet, soulful piece from a forgotten artist, began to fill the room.

Rhys's gaze flickered to the radio, a small, bewildered smile on his face. "A radio? I didn't think you'd pack a radio."

Finn's lips, a hard, taut line, softened. "It was a gift from an old friend. A little something for when the silence gets to be too much."

Rhys looked at him, a silent question in his eyes. He slowly slid off the cot, his bare feet making no sound on the dusty concrete floor. He walked to the center of the room, his movements slow and deliberate. He held out a hand, a small, vulnerable gesture. "Finn Kage. The rogue agent. The man with the heart of a ghost. Would you... would you like to dance with me?"

The question was a direct challenge to the man Finn had always been. A man of protocol, of rules, of cold detachment. But the man he was now, a man in a cold, sterile room with a small, beautiful omega and a new life growing inside him, was a different creature altogether. He rose slowly, his powerful frame a dark, imposing shadow in the dim light. He took Rhys's hand, his touch a gentle, hesitant thing.

They began to dance. Not with the frantic, passionate fire of their first night together, but with a slow, tender grace. Finn's hands rested on Rhys's waist, his powerful fingers a gentle, supporting weight. Rhys's arms, soft and fragile, draped over Finn's shoulders, his hands a gentle, reassuring touch on the back of his neck. They swayed to the slow, soulful rhythm of the music, their bodies moving in a perfect, unspoken harmony.

The dance was a small, precious moment of normalcy, a fragile, beautiful illusion in the heart of their chaotic reality. The scent of rain and sandalwood, now a soft, intoxicating perfume, filled Finn's senses. He looked into Rhys's eyes, a deep, liquid brown, and he saw not the face of a victim, but the face of a survivor. He saw a man who had been pushed to the edge, who had lost everything, but who had not broken. He saw a man who was now, against all odds, a partner.

"Finn," Rhys said, his voice a low, barely-there whisper. "What will we do? We have no home. We have no money. We have no future. We're ghosts. We're nothing."

Finn's hand, which had been resting on Rhys's waist, moved slowly, deliberately, to his stomach. The touch was a gentle, reverent thing, a silent, powerful acknowledgment of the life within.

"We're not nothing," Finn said, his voice a low, guttural murmur that vibrated through Rhys's body. "We're a family. We have each other. We have our child. We will build a future. It won't be the one we wanted. It won't be a house with a picket fence and a dog. But it will be a future. A new life. A new home. I promise you."

The words were not just a promise; they were a vow. He looked into Rhys's eyes, into the deep, liquid brown of his gaze, and he saw a flicker of hope. A small, fragile light in the darkness. He leaned in, his lips a gentle, soft pressure on Rhys's. This kiss was a world away from the desperation of their first. There was no frantic, primal hunger. There was no desperate need. There was only tenderness. There was only hope.

The kiss deepened, a slow, tender exploration of their new, fragile bond. Their shared breath was a warm, sweet perfume in the cold, sterile air. Finn's hands moved slowly, deliberately, over Rhys's body, a gentle, reassuring touch that promised a lifetime of protection.

Just as the kiss deepened, as the moment of fragile, beautiful normalcy solidified into a tangible truth, a sudden, sharp jolt shot through Rhys's body. It was a strange, unfamiliar sensation, a low, buzzing hum that started in the pit of his stomach and radiated outward, a subtle, electrical current that made every hair on his body stand on end. He pulled back, his eyes wide and bewildered.

"What's wrong?" Finn asked, his voice a low, concerned growl.

Rhys's hand, a small, trembling thing, moved to his stomach, a protective, questioning touch. "I... I don't know. It's... a feeling. A shift. Something's happening. I can feel it. It's moving. The pregnancy... it's moving faster. Something's wrong."

The words were a brutal, terrifying reality check. The hopeful, fragile moment of peace shattered into a thousand pieces. The ticking clock of their new life, a clock they had foolishly believed had more time on it, was now a loud, insistent scream. Finn's face, which had been soft and tender, hardened into a mask of grim determination. He was an agent again, his mind racing through possibilities, resources, and dangers.

They stood there, in the heart of the sterile, unforgiving safe house, a small, shivering knot of hopeful dread. The quiet moment of peace was gone, replaced by the cold, hard reality of their situation. The peaceful melody of the radio was a cruel, ironic counterpoint to the ticking clock of Rhys's pregnancy, a time bomb that was now a tangible, physical weight between them. Their small moment of normalcy, a fragile, tender illusion, was now a distant memory, overshadowed by the terrifying, life-altering truth that their new reality, and their unborn child, was on a fast and terrifying track. The hunt had begun, but they were now racing against not just a ruthless crime boss and a compromised federal agency, but against time itself.

Chapter 9

The Ghost in the Machine

The laptop was a black, sterile sentinel on the rusted metal table, a beacon of purpose in the heart of the desolate safe house. It was a piece of Finn's old life, a hardened, secure machine designed for infiltration and data extraction, stripped of all personal markings and connected to the outside world only through a labyrinthine series of encrypted proxy servers. Its cold, unforgiving light cast a halo on Rhys's face as he sat before it, the screen a window into the life he had so meticulously documented and, until now, believed he had escaped.

He had been at it for hours. The process was a painstaking, almost trance-like ritual. He would close his eyes, allowing his photographic memory to conjure the raw data—the flickering green numbers of a ledger entry, the cold, black text of an offshore transaction, the date of a shipment, the name of a shell company. It was a mental excavation, a deep, systematic dig into a mountain of information he had stored, organized, and cataloged over a lifetime. He would then open his eyes, the memory still burning bright behind his eyelids, and type, his fingers a blur of motion over the keyboard, recreating the ledgers line by line, page by page. The faint click-clack of the keys was a constant, hypnotic sound in the otherwise silent room.

Finn watched him from his perch on the cot, his gun, a cold, comforting weight, resting on his knee. The sight was a constant, surreal contradiction. The omega, once a silent, unassuming fixture in the background of a criminal empire, was now the ghost in the machine. He was the key, the weapon, the living embodiment of everything Finn had been hunting. And now, as he watched him work, as he saw the deep, concentrated focus on Rhys's face, Finn felt a strange, new sensation—a grudging admiration mixed with a powerful, protective instinct. Rhys wasn't just a survivor. He was a force of nature.

The ledgers began to take shape, a sprawling digital web of corruption and crime that painted a damning picture of the Petrov family's enterprise. They were not just a criminal organization; they were a financial empire built on a foundation of money laundering, human trafficking, and illicit arms deals. The numbers, cold and unforgiving, were a testament to their ruthlessness. As the data accumulated, as the connections became clearer, a grim, determined fire burned in Finn's gray eyes. The mission was no longer an abstract idea. It was a tangible, digital reality, a weapon they could use to bring Dimitri's world crashing down.

Rhys's fingers, which had been a constant blur of motion, suddenly stopped. His head tilted slightly, his eyes, wide and focused, stared at the screen. There was a faint, almost imperceptible tremor in his hand.

"What is it?" Finn asked, his voice low and guttural. The change in Rhys's posture, the sudden stillness, was a red flag. He was no longer just recreating data. He was seeing something new. Something he hadn't expected.

"The shell corporations," Rhys said, his voice a low, raspy sound. "There's a small, dormant account. It's a ghost company, a phantom. I remember it. It's not in the ledgers. It was a different kind of project. Something... secret. Something my father only ever mentioned once. I thought it was a contingency plan for a failed business deal." He turned to look at Finn, his eyes wide with a dawning, terrible realization. "But it's not a contingency plan. It's a back-end server. A hidden directory. I can feel it. It's a phantom in the machine. It's not meant to be found."

The words sent a cold, sharp jolt of alarm through Finn. The scent of a trap was a familiar one, a subtle, musky perfume on the wind. He rose from the cot, his movements quick and fluid, and walked to Rhys's side. He looked at the screen. The directory was hidden within a series of encrypted sub-files, a deep, dark corner of the Petrov servers that was accessible only with the most precise, unyielding knowledge of the system. Rhys, with his photographic memory and his intimate knowledge of the family's systems, was the only person who could have ever found it.

"Can you open it?" Finn asked, his voice a low, terse command.

Rhys shook his head, a small, frustrated movement. "No. The password... it's not a normal password. It's a key. A unique biometric key. It's tied to Dimitri's DNA. It's a dead man's switch. If he dies, the file is automatically released. If someone tries to open it without his key, it is automatically released. It's... a fail-safe."

Finn's hand, which had been resting on Rhys's shoulder, tightened into a steel vice. His mind, a cold, analytical machine, began to work through the possibilities. The security system. The protocol. The risk. This was not just a threat. It was a poison. A self-destruct mechanism. A final, unforgiving act of revenge.

Rhys's hands, trembling now, typed a few commands into the terminal. A small, black box appeared on the screen, a series of cryptic, coded messages flashing across its surface.

"What is that?" Finn asked, his voice a low, dangerous growl.

"I'm running a low-level decryption algorithm," Rhys said, his voice a whisper, his gaze fixed on the screen. "It's not enough to open the file, but it's enough to get a glimpse. A single line of code. A single piece of metadata."

The screen flashed. A single line of text, a stark, uncompromising truth, appeared on the screen, a final, definitive answer to their unspoken questions.

```
PAYLOAD:       R_KAGE_FBI_IDENTITY.zip          |
DESTINATION:   .darkweb/Petrov_Alliance.net     |
TRIGGER: SIGINT_01
```

Rhys's head turned slowly, his eyes meeting Finn's. The words, so cold and professional, were a brutal, devastating reality. He didn't need to explain the code. Finn understood it.

"The Kage identity… is you," Rhys said, his voice a low, trembling whisper. "He knew. He's had it for a long time. He's been waiting."

The words were a brutal, physical blow. Finn's entire life, his career, his identity… it had all been a lie, a fabricated persona designed to protect him in the field. But Dimitri, the ruthless and paranoid head of the Petrov family, had been one step ahead. He had not just documented his own crimes. He had documented Finn's life. He had created a weapon, a poison, a silent, deadly threat that was waiting to be released.

The stakes, which had been a low, rumbling hum of danger, now screamed with a furious, unrelenting intensity. Capturing Dimitri wasn't enough. It was a death sentence. It was a guaranteed, public, and brutal end for the man who was now, against all odds, Rhys's partner. They had to neutralize the switch. They had to get the file. And they had to do it in a way that left no digital trace, no sign of their interference.

They stared at the screen, a small, shivering knot of hopeful dread in the cold, sterile room. The laptop, once a beacon of hope, was now a digital time bomb. The hunt had begun, but they were now racing against not just a ruthless crime boss and a compromised federal agency, but against a ghost in the machine, a silent, deadly contingency plan that would erase them both from existence if they made a single misstep. The game had changed. And the stakes had just become immeasurably higher.

Chapter 10

The Betrayal

The decision to contact Agent Ramirez was not made lightly. It was a desperate, Hail Mary of a plan, born from the crushing weight of their isolation. She was Finn's former partner, a tough, no-nonsense alpha with a deep-seated code of honor and an almost maternal instinct for the agents she mentored. She had been the one to teach Finn how to read a room, how to trust his gut, how to be more than just a ghost in the machine. If there was anyone left in the FBI who would listen, who would believe his story, it was her.

Using the secure laptop and a series of rotating burner phones, Finn crafted a coded message—a series of phrases only they would understand—and sent it to a long-dormant secure channel he knew she monitored. He didn't include the ledgers or the "dead man's switch" file in the message. He knew the risk was too great. The message was simple, a desperate plea for a meeting, a promise of information that would "break the case wide open." It was a fishing line cast into a black ocean, a desperate hope that she would bite.

He watched the clock, the digital numbers a relentless reminder of the ticking time bomb in Rhys's womb. Every hour that passed felt like a week. He saw the flicker of hope in Rhys's eyes every time he checked the screen, and the fragile, beautiful hope broke Finn's heart. He was putting all of their faith in a system that had already branded him a rogue, a traitor, a ghost. But they had no other choice. They were running out of time, running out of resources, and most importantly, running out of hope.

The response came twelve hours later. A coded message, a short, terse affirmation of the rendezvous.

"Meeting point is the old Chicago freight yards. Near the abandoned grain silo. Midnight. Alone."

Finn's sharp, gray eyes narrowed, a cold, analytical fire burning in their depths. The old freight yards. It was a perfect meeting spot—isolated, full of shadows, and with multiple entry and exit points. It was a location they had used in training simulations, a place they both knew intimately. The scent of ozone, rust, and rain was a comforting, familiar perfume on the wind.

As they drove to the meeting point in the dead of the night, the stolen car rattling and groaning over the uneven pavement, a nervous energy filled the air. Rhys, a small, fragile knot of tension in the passenger seat, kept his hands pressed to his stomach, a protective, questioning touch. He had not questioned the decision to contact Ramirez. He had simply trusted Finn, a quiet, heartbreaking faith that was both a shield and a terrible weight on Finn's shoulders.

The freight yards were a sprawling, desolate graveyard of forgotten machinery. The air was thick with the scent of rust and decay, a cold, unforgiving perfume. The abandoned grain silo, a massive, cylindrical tomb of concrete and steel, rose against the black sky, a silent sentinel in the gloom. Finn parked the car a few hundred yards away, killed the engine, and turned to Rhys.

"Stay here," he commanded, his voice a low, fierce murmur. "Don't move. Don't make a sound. I'll be back."

Rhys's hand, a small, trembling thing, reached out and gently touched his arm. "Be careful," he whispered, his eyes wide and pleading in the darkness.

Finn gave him a small, grim smile, a reassurance he couldn't yet feel. "Always."

He slipped out of the car, his movements quick and fluid, a ghost returning to his old hunting grounds. He moved through the shadows, his senses on high alert. The scent of rain and dust filled his nose. He could hear the faint, rhythmic drumming of a distant freight train. The silence was a living, breathing thing. He was a predator in his element.

Then, he saw it. A familiar, dark sedan, a Honda Accord he had seen Ramirez drive a hundred times. It was parked a few yards from the grain silo, its headlights off, its presence a stark, unmistakable beacon of hope. His heart, which had been a cold, methodical machine, warmed with a cautious, fragile flicker of hope. She was here. She had come. He wasn't alone.

But as he moved closer, a faint, discordant scent caught his attention—a subtle, musky perfume of cheap aftershave and stale cigar smoke. It was the scent of Dimitri's men. A cold, brutal shock, a physical punch to the gut, slammed into him. The scent was old, dried, like a lingering ghost on the wind. The car was empty. Ramirez wasn't there.

"It's a trap," he whispered to the shadows, the words a raw, guttural growl. He had been so blind, so desperate, so willing to believe in the ghost of his old life, that he had walked right into it. The coded message. The rendezvous. The familiar car. It was all a carefully constructed lie. Dimitri had a mole. Someone in the FBI had known about the message, had intercepted it, had given them up.

A sudden, sharp sound, the metallic click of a rifle bolt, echoed through the silence. A group of men, dark, imposing figures with guns drawn, emerged from the shadows. They were not FBI. They were not agents. They were Dimitri's men. A cold, hard knot of fear, of a fear not for himself, but for Rhys, tightened in Finn's gut.

The game had changed. The rules were gone. This was not a negotiation. This was an ambush.

"Finn Kage," a voice, a low, guttural murmur, echoed through the silence. "The ghost. Come out. We know you're here. We know about the omega. We know about the child. Don't make this difficult."

The words were a direct, brutal threat. They were not just here for him. They were here for Rhys. They were here for their child. The cold, analytical part of Finn's brain, the part that had been an agent for so long, was gone, replaced by a primal, fierce, protective instinct. He was no longer an agent. He was an alpha.

He opened fire. The sound of the gunshot, a sharp, deafening crack, shattered the silence. The flash of the muzzle, a brief, violent burst of light, illuminated the faces of the men, a map of cruel, predatory smiles. He fired again, then ducked behind a stack of rusted steel barrels, the bullets zipping past his head with a high-pitched, metallic whine. He was outmatched. Outgunned. They had a rifle. He had a handgun.

He was fighting a desperate, losing battle, a frenzied ballet of violence and survival, when a sharp, searing pain exploded in his left side. A burning, fiery sensation that made his body flinch, his breath catch in his throat. He looked down. A dark, blooming stain was spreading across the fabric of his shirt. A bullet. A clean, neat hole that was now a furious, agonizing burn.

The pain, a sharp, white-hot fire, was a shock to his system. He stumbled back, his body hitting the steel barrels with a metallic clang. He slid down, his back against the cold, unforgiving steel, his gun still raised, his mind a roaring furnace of pain and a primal, desperate need to protect.

A sudden, sharp sound, the click of a car door, drew his attention. Rhys. He had disobeyed his command. He had come out. He was here. He was a small, trembling figure in the darkness, but his gaze was fixed on Finn. He was not a bystander. He was a partner.

"Finn!" Rhys's voice was a low, terrified whisper, but there was an unyielding strength in it that cut through the roaring chaos. He moved toward him, his hands, a small, fragile blur of motion, reaching out to help. He grabbed Finn's arm, his touch a gentle, steadying force that grounded him in the midst of the chaos.

"Get back," Finn said, his voice a low, pained growl. "Get back now."

But Rhys didn't. He helped him up, his body a small, fragile support against Finn's powerful, wounded frame. They began to run, a desperate, hobbling flight through the shadows. The sound of the men, their boots thudding against the pavement, their angry, guttural shouts, grew closer. The air was thick with the scent of their rage, their victory, their alpha scent.

They scrambled back to the car, a frantic, two-person retreat. Rhys fumbled with the keys, his hands shaking so violently he almost dropped them. He got the door open, helped Finn into the driver's seat, and slid into the passenger seat himself. He fumbled with the key in the ignition, his hands a blur of motion, and the engine, a low, guttural roar, came to life.

As they sped away, the tires squealing in protest, the headlights of the black sedan a distant, menacing beacon in the rearview mirror, a final, definitive truth settled on them both. The FBI was gone. The hope for institutional help, for a safe return, for a resolution… it was gone. Ramirez had either been compromised, or she had been the mole all along. There was no one left to trust. There was only them. Wounded, exhausted, and bleeding in the dark. Their plan, a desperate, fragile thing, was in tatters. They were truly on their own.

Chapter 11

The Ticking Clock

The safe house, a forgotten cell in the city's underbelly, was a sanctuary of cold, sterile quiet that had been brutally invaded by the clamor of pain and fear. The air, once just a mix of dust and disuse, now carried the potent, coppery tang of Finn's blood and the sharp, visceral scent of Rhys's terror. Finn sat on the floor, his broad back pressed against the unforgiving concrete wall, his breath coming in ragged, shallow gasps. The bullet wound in his left side was no longer just a hole; it was a living, breathing fire, a white-hot furnace that radiated agony through his powerful frame with every beat of his heart. The makeshift bandage—a torn strip of his shirt—was a flimsy barrier against the flow, already stained a deep crimson. The pain was a constant, vicious reminder of their failed rendezvous, the one last glimmer of hope that had been extinguished with a single pull of a trigger.

He pressed a hand to the wound, his fingers a clumsy, trembling shield against the fiery burn. The raw, searing pain made his head swim, the world tilting on its axis. He felt a deep, profound helplessness, a sensation he had not known since his earliest days as an agent. He was a weapon, a finely tuned machine of violence and survival, and yet, here, now, he was reduced to a bleeding man on a cold floor, his body a fragile, broken thing. He was a protector whose own body had failed him, a guardian who was now a burden.

The thought was a more bitter, more agonizing pain than the bullet wound itself.

Across from him, on the narrow cot, Rhys was a small, shivering knot of humanity. The past forty-eight hours had taken a cruel toll. The frantic flight, the ceaseless fear, the raw, emotional shock of Finn's confession and subsequent betrayal had stripped him of his defenses. His body, once a vessel of quiet endurance, was now a battlefield of its own. He was hunched over, his hands clutched to his stomach, a protective, questioning touch against the sharp, jarring movements within. The baby, which had been a gentle, reassuring flutter, was now a furious storm in his womb, its kicks and turns sharp and insistent. It wasn't a baby anymore; it was a ticking clock, and the ticking was a rhythm of pure, unadulterated terror.

"It hurts," Rhys whispered, his voice a small, pained sound that scraped against the silence. "Finn, it hurts so bad."

Finn, his face a pale, strained mask, pushed himself up from the floor, his movements slow and deliberate against the searing protest of his wound. He crawled to Rhys's side, the effort sending a fresh wave of agony through him. He reached out and gently touched Rhys's forehead. It was slick with sweat, his body radiating a feverish heat. He was a protector, an alpha whose entire life had been defined by his ability to defend and neutralize threats, and yet here, now, he was utterly helpless. He couldn't heal him. He couldn't protect him from this. He could only watch as the natural, rhythmic contractions of the womb, a process he knew only from the abstract, clinical reports of his mission files, became a terrible, living reality.

He didn't need a medical degree to know what was happening. The signs were undeniable. The constant, low-level ache was now a sharp, rhythmic contraction. The fever. The frantic, desperate movements of the baby. Rhys was going into labor. The pregnancy, which should have been a secret, a quiet, beautiful miracle, had become a ticking clock, and the clock was running out of time.

"How… how long has it been?" Finn's voice was a low, pained growl. He had lost track of the hours, the days, the minutes. Time had become a meaningless blur.

"Since… since the first one?" Rhys's voice was a breathless, pained gasp. "I don't know. An hour? The pain… it just keeps getting worse." His hands, a small, trembling shield, pressed down on his swollen belly. "The baby… it's so angry. It won't stop moving."

A new kind of fire—a cold, grim, determined fire— began to burn in Finn's gray eyes. The ambush, the betrayal, the pain… it had all been a test. A test he had failed. He had put his faith in a system that had abandoned him. He had placed his hope in a ghost of an ally who had turned out to be a monster. He had been chasing the wrong game, playing by the wrong rules.

The rules were gone. The game had changed. He wasn't going to play it anymore. He was going to break it.

"The ledgers," Finn said, his voice a low, fierce murmur. "The 'dead man's switch' file. We can't use them to negotiate. We can't use them as leverage. We can't trust anyone inside the system."

Rhys, his face contorted in a fresh spasm of pain, looked at him, his eyes wide and pleading. "Then what do we do? We can't just… we can't just give up."

Finn's hand, a rough, calloused thing, reached out and gently touched Rhys's face, his thumb stroking his damp cheek. "We don't give up. We use them as a weapon. A nuclear bomb. We don't send them to the FBI. We don't send them to a single agent. We send them to everyone. We expose Dimitri's empire to the world. We force the FBI's hand. We force them to act. We force them to choose between their corrupt mole and the public outrage of the world watching them fail."

The plan was insane. It was audacious. It was brilliant. It was the only way. It was a desperate, final, unforgiving act of revenge. They had nothing left to lose. Their lives were already forfeit. Their hope was already gone. But they had the truth. They had the numbers. They had the ledgers. And they had a laptop and a desperate, determined will to survive.

Working through the night, their movements a frantic, desperate blur of motion, they began to assemble the digital package. Finn, his face pale and haggard, a cold, grim determination in his eyes, sat on the floor, the laptop balanced on his knees. He was no longer just an agent. He was a father. A partner. A protector. He was a force of nature in his own right. Rhys, his body wracked with pain, was a ghost in the machine again, his fingers a blur over the keyboard. He was a force of nature, a quiet, formidable survivor who was defying the crushing weight of his physical pain to complete their mission.

Rhys's eyes, a brilliant, terrifying blue, were glazed over with pain, but his mind was sharp, his photographic memory a powerful, unwavering beacon in the storm. He would close his eyes, a pained grimace on his face, and then, in a voice that was a mix of a gasp and a low, breathless command, he would recite a string of numbers. "Shell company eight-four-two-seven-five, established November twelfth, two-thousand-seventeen. Transaction amount, thirty-seven million. Recipient account, Alpha-niner-three-one-four, Cyprus. It's a ghost company for the arms deals." Finn would type, his fingers a blur of motion, his mind a racing labyrinth of data entry, his gaze never leaving Rhys's face.

They organized the ledgers into a clear, concise narrative of Dimitri's criminal empire. They annotated the data, adding notes and a comprehensive, bullet-point list of the Petrovs' crimes. They even included a small, cryptic, coded message to the FBI's official media account—a short, terse accusation that would send a shockwave of panic through the bureau. It was a perfect, beautiful trap. It was a self-destruct mechanism that would bring Dimitri's world crashing down.

As the hours bled into a new, anxious dawn, Rhys's contractions became more frequent, more intense, a slow, methodical march toward the inevitable. He would cry out, a low, guttural sound of pain, and Finn would stop, his fingers hovering over the keyboard, his face a mask of profound helplessness. He would reach out, his hand a comforting weight on Rhys's shoulder, and whisper a low, fierce promise. "Almost there. Just a little longer, we're almost there."

Just as the final file was being compressed, just as the final email was being written, a low, guttural cry of pain escaped Rhys's lips. It was a raw, primal sound that cut through the silence, a sound that made Finn's blood run cold. He turned, his heart a frantic, furious drum against his ribs.

Rhys's body was wracked with a new, agonizing spasm, a convulsion of pure, unadulterated pain. His hands, which had been a blur of motion over the keyboard, were now clasped to his stomach, a tight, protective grip.

"Finn," he whispered, his voice a small, desperate sound. "It's… it's time."

A wave of warm liquid, a final, definitive truth, flowed over the cot, a dark, spreading stain on the worn canvas. The water had broken. The ticking clock of Rhys's pregnancy was gone, replaced by the immediate, overwhelming, and life-altering reality of labor. The baby was coming. Now.

A sudden, jarring sound, a low, guttural hum that was a hundred times more terrifying than a gunshot, echoed through the silence. Vehicles. So many vehicles. The scent of gasoline and cheap cigar smoke, the musky, dominant perfume of Dimitri's men, filled the air. They were outside. They had found them. The safe house, their last sanctuary, their last hope, was surrounded. The wail of a hundred engines, the angry, determined murmur of a hundred men, filled the air. The trap had been sprung. But they weren't the ones in it. The hunt was over. The siege had begun.

Chapter 12

Cornered

The low hum began as a vibration in the concrete floor, a subterranean tremor that sent a shiver through the worn canvas of the cot. It was not the isolated drone of a single car, but the deep, throaty chorus of an approaching swarm. The sound grew, a grinding, metallic groan of tires over cracked asphalt and the guttural roar of powerful engines, a symphony of menace that swallowed the fragile silence of the safe house. Headlights, brutal and unforgiving, began to slice through the grime-streaked window, painting fleeting, phantom-like shadows on the bare walls—the silhouettes of a world closing in. The smell of exhaust, a foul, acidic perfume, began to seep through the ventilation grates, fouling the air. The siege had begun.

Finn, his body a tight, coiled spring of pain and adrenaline, pushed himself up from the floor, his wounded side a searing, white-hot protest. He pressed a hand to the wound, his fingers a clumsy, trembling shield against the fiery burn. The raw, searing pain made his head swim, the world tilting on its axis. He felt a deep, profound helplessness, a sensation he had not known since his earliest days as an agent. He was a weapon, a finely tuned machine of violence and survival, and yet, here, now, he was reduced to a bleeding man on a cold floor, his body a fragile, broken thing. He was a protector whose own body had failed him, a guardian who was now a burden. The thought was a more bitter, more agonizing pain than the bullet wound itself.

The frantic thrum of the engines was a familiar, primal beat. He was no longer a bleeding, desperate man on a cold floor; he was a cornered animal, his alpha instincts, so long suppressed by the rigid protocols of his life, now screaming through his veins. He limped to the window, his movements a series of sharp, decisive actions. He didn't need to see to know. The number of vehicles, the relentless, coordinated approach, was a tell-tale signature of Dimitri's full force. The Petrov family was not sending a warning; they were coming for a massacre.

He turned from the window, his gray eyes, usually so sharp and cold, now burning with a raw, protective fire. Rhys lay on the cot, his body a map of trembling tension, a pained whimper escaping his lips. The rhythmic, insistent waves of pain were now a constant presence, each one a gasp of breathless agony. His hands, small and trembling, were clenched into fists, knuckles white as he fought to contain the storm raging within his body. The scent of his fear, a potent, coppery tang, filled the air, mingling with the bitter perfume of Finn's own rising anger.

"They're here," Rhys whispered, his voice a small, fragile thing, a question he already knew the answer to.

Finn didn't speak. He moved, his body a graceful, broken shadow in the dim light. He checked the lone, steel-reinforced door, the rusted hinges, the bolted lock—all of it a futile, meaningless gesture. They were not designed to hold against an assault of this magnitude. This was not a fortress; it was a tomb. His gaze swept the room, searching for a phantom escape route that didn't exist. The weight of his helplessness was a physical burden, heavier than the bullet wound in his side.

A new sound, distinct from the drone of the engines, cut through the air—the methodical, deliberate crunch of leather soles on gravel. It was a single, measured rhythm, an arrival that was meant to be noted. A car door, a single, sharp clack of a high-end sedan, echoed with a finality that brooked no argument. Then, the sound of a voice, amplified by the sterile quiet of the approaching dawn, filled the air.

"Finn Kage," the voice boomed, its tone a low, guttural murmur that resonated with an unmistakable triumph. "Or should I say, Agent Shadow. I've been waiting for you to come out and play."

Dimitri Petrov. The silver-streaked hair, the impeccably tailored suit that hid the formidable, aging power beneath, the cold, calculating eyes—Finn could see him in his mind's eye as clearly as if he were standing in the room. He was a force of nature, a ruthless predator who had built his empire on a foundation of violence and manipulation. He was here now, a wolf come to the door of his old hunting grounds.

"The smell of your fear is intoxicating, my boy," Dimitri continued, his voice a low, taunting purr. "And the scent of the little omega... delicious. I always wondered what would happen if a man with your... suppressed nature... found a home in the heart of my family. It was a fascinating little experiment."

The words were a brutal, physical blow. Finn's entire life, his career, his identity, his quiet, simmering love for Rhys—it had all been a game to this man. A little experiment. Dimitri's arrogance was a tangible, palpable force, a suffocating presence that filled the small room.

Rhys's body, which had been a tight, trembling knot of pain, suddenly went still. A contraction, a wave of agonizing fire, seized him, but this time, he did not cry out. He bit down on his bottom lip, a small, pained grimace on his face, but his eyes, a brilliant, terrifying blue, were now fixed on the door. The fear was gone, burned away by a cold, searing defiance. This was not just a threat to his life; it was an insult to his very existence. Dimitri's casual cruelty, his dismissal of their love as a mere 'experiment,' was the final straw.

"You're a coward, Dimitri," Rhys's voice was a low, pained gasp, but there was a new, hard edge to it, an uncompromising steel that made Finn's blood run cold. "You're a relic. A ghost. Your empire is built on lies, on fear, and on the bones of men you tricked into believing you were a god. You're nothing but a man with a fragile, little ego, and I'm going to watch it all burn down."

The words, a raw, unfiltered expression of the truth, were a direct, brutal challenge. The voice outside went silent for a moment, a moment of profound, uncomprehending shock. Then, a low, cruel laugh, a sound like glass shattering, echoed through the silence.

"Such fire, my little omega," Dimitri said, his voice laced with a new, dangerous edge of fury. "Such defiance. It's a shame your life is about to end. But you're right. My empire is a symphony of lies, and you… you were my conductor." The laughter faded, replaced by a cold, hard voice. "But the concert is over. Now, the music will die."

Finn's hand, a rough, calloused thing, moved to his gun. The pain in his side was forgotten, eclipsed by a primal, furious rage. The controlled, protocol-driven agent was gone, replaced by the alpha, the protector, the furious guardian of his mate and his unborn child. He looked at Dimitri's face in his mind's eye, no longer as a target, but as a beast, a monster, a cancer he had to cut out of their lives for good.

He turned to Rhys, his gaze a silent, fierce promise. He reached out and touched his hand, their fingers intertwining in a desperate, final grasp.

"I won't let them touch you," Finn said, his voice a low, guttural murmur that vibrated with a raw, undeniable emotion. "I swear to you. I won't let them."

Rhys met his gaze, his eyes a brilliant, terrifying blue in the dim light. The pain, the fear, the exhaustion... it was all there, but beneath it, a defiant, unbreakable resolve burned bright. He knew. He knew this was the end. But he also knew that their love, their fragile, beautiful bond, was a truth that Dimitri could never kill.

A new sound, the sharp, metallic click of a rifle bolt, echoed through the silence. Dimitri's voice, a cold, hard command, filled the air. "Inside. Now."

The silence stretched, a terrifying, drawn-out moment of stillness before the storm. The sound of boots, a hundred of them, thudding on the concrete, grew closer. The air was thick with the scent of their rage, their victory, their primal, dominant alpha scents. The door, a flimsy barrier of wood and metal, was about to break.

Finn rose, his body a magnificent, broken machine of muscle and bone. He moved to the center of the room, his movements a slow, deliberate dance of a man preparing to die. He stood with his back to Rhys, his gun raised, his body a living, breathing shield. He was ready.

Rhys, his body wracked with a new, agonizing spasm of pain, pushed himself up from the cot. He stood, his movements slow and agonizing, his body a small, fragile beacon of defiance in the dim light. He stood with his back to Finn, his hands a protective shield over his stomach, his gaze fixed on the door. He was ready.

They stood there, back to back, a final, beautiful portrait of a broken, defiant love. The sound of the men, a low, angry murmur, grew closer. The scent of their rage, their victory, their dominant alpha scents filled the air. The final moment of peace was over. The storm had arrived.

Chapter 13

The Final Stand

The door, a flimsy barrier of wood and metal, groaned under the weight of the assault, the hinges screaming a protest that was drowned out by the splintering thud of a battering ram. The wood splintered, the lock gave way with a final, desperate CRACK, and a torrent of men, dark, imposing figures with guns drawn, poured into the room. The air was a maelstrom of sound, light, and motion—the crash of splintered wood, the flashlights cutting through the gloom, the low, guttural shouts of men on the hunt. The small, sterile safe house was instantly transformed into a brutal, claustrophobic battlefield.

Finn, his body a magnificent, broken machine of muscle and bone, was a blur of motion. He moved with a primal, furious grace, his gun a silent, deadly extension of his will. He was no longer an agent fighting for a mission; he was an alpha fighting for his mate and his child. He fired, his shots precise and unforgiving, a desperate, final act of defense. The men, surprised by his ferocity, fell back, a few of them crumpling to the floor with low, pained groans. But more came. A relentless, unstoppable wave of violence.

Dimitri, a magnificent, triumphant figure in his tailored suit, watched from the doorway, his face a cold, triumphant mask. He was a conductor, and this was his symphony of death. He was not just here to kill Finn; he was here to watch him die, to watch the final, desperate struggle of a man who had dared to challenge him.

A new, agonizing sound, a low, guttural cry of pain, escaped Rhys's lips. The battle, the chaos, the frantic, life-or-death struggle—it all faded into a distant murmur. The contractions, a series of white-hot spasms, seized his body, twisting and tearing with a force that made his vision swim. He collapsed to the floor, his body a small, broken thing on the cold concrete. He was a survivor, a warrior, but his body was betraying him.

Finn, in the middle of a brutal, hand-to-hand fight with one of Dimitri's men, saw him fall. The sight, a raw, devastating image of his mate in agony, sent a new, furious surge of adrenaline through his system. The alpha, the protector, the furious guardian, roared to life. He broke the man's hold with a vicious twist of his wrist, slammed his fist into his jaw with a sickening CRUNCH, and turned, his gaze fixed on Dimitri.

The fight with Dimitri was not a battle; it was a primal, brutal display of raw strength and rage. They met in the center of the room, a whirlwind of muscle and bone, their bodies a blur of motion. Dimitri, a powerful, aging alpha, was a formidable opponent, his movements a series of calculated, vicious blows. He was a hunter, a predator, a man who had built his empire on a foundation of violence, and his rage was a tangible, physical force.

But Finn was not just an agent anymore. He was a father. A protector. He was fighting for a new life, for a future, for a fragile, beautiful bond that Dimitri could never comprehend. He met Dimitri's blows with a desperate, furious strength, his body a living, breathing shield. He was a man who had nothing left to lose, and that made him more dangerous than any weapon.

Rhys, his body a battlefield of pure, unadulterated agony, was on the cot, his hands pressed to his stomach, a protective, desperate touch. The contractions were coming faster now, a relentless, unstoppable storm of pain. But in the midst of the chaos, in the roaring furnace of his body, his mind, his one last weapon, was still a cold, methodical machine.

He closed his eyes, allowing his photographic memory, a mental library of a thousand forgotten details, to conjure the raw data. The ledgers. The 'dead man's switch' file. It was all there, a sprawling, intricate map of Dimitri's lies. But there was one last piece of the puzzle, one last piece of information he had never shared, a final, devastating truth that could bring the whole empire crashing down.

"Finn!" Rhys's voice was a low, guttural shriek, a raw, primal cry that cut through the roaring chaos of the battle. "The backup! The real ledgers! They're not on the server! They're hidden! In the… the foundation of the old warehouse! The one by the river! Under the… under the concrete! The code… the code is… the code is my brother's birthday! Finn, please! You have to send it!"

The words, a raw, unfiltered expression of the truth, were a lightning bolt in the storm. The final piece of the puzzle. The one last detail that could expose Dimitri's entire empire to the world. Finn, his body a battlefield of bruises and blood, heard him. The alpha, the protector, the father, heard him.

He met Dimitri's vicious blow with a furious, desperate strength, his body a shield, his mind a racing, methodical labyrinth of new information. He slammed his fist into Dimitri's jaw with a sickening CRUNCH, the blow a final, definitive declaration of his victory. Dimitri's eyes, cold and calculating, went wide with shock and pain. His body, a powerful, aging thing, crumpled to the floor, a broken, defeated shadow of his former self.

The battle was over. The silence, a terrifying, blessed relief, fell over the room. Finn, his body a magnificent, broken machine of muscle and bone, stood over Dimitri's still form, his chest heaving, his gun lowered, his mind a racing labyrinth of his new victory. He had done it. He had won.

Just as the silence settled, a new sound, the sharp, authoritative shout of a woman, broke through the gloom. "FBI! Hands up!"

The door, a shattered, splintered thing, was suddenly filled with a torrent of light and motion. Agent Ramirez, a formidable figure in her tactical gear, her face a mask of grim determination, stood in the doorway. She was a beacon of hope in the darkness. She held a single, printed piece of paper in her hand—a copy of the email. Finn's final, desperate act of defiance. The final, devastating truth.

Finn's gaze, which had been fixed on the body of his defeated enemy, now fell to Rhys. He was on the cot, his body a small, broken thing, his face a mask of pure, unadulterated pain. The baby. The ticking clock. The real battle was just beginning.

He dropped his gun, the metal a cold, meaningless weight, and ran to Rhys's side. He knelt on the floor, his wounded body a useless, broken thing, his hands, a rough, calloused touch, reaching out to Rhys's face.

"I'm here," Finn said, his voice a low, raw whisper, a desperate, final vow. "I'm here, my love. I'm here. We're safe. We're safe."

Rhys's eyes, a brilliant, terrifying blue, opened. He looked at Finn, at the broken, bleeding figure of his alpha, his protector, his love. He smiled, a small, pained, beautiful flash of emotion. "You did it," he whispered, his voice a small, raw sound. "You won."

And in that moment, in the midst of the chaos, in the heart of the battlefield, Finn and Rhys were a world away. The sirens, a low, mournful wail, grew closer. The shouts of the FBI agents, the sounds of their methodical movements, the flashlights cutting through the gloom—it all faded into a distant murmur. The only thing that mattered was the two of them, their hands intertwined, their bodies a small, fragile knot of love and survival. Finn's duty, a cold, methodical machine of justice, and his love, a fierce, protective fire, had finally converged. The battle was over. The new life, their new life, had begun.

Chapter 14

New Beginnings

The air, thick with the acrid scent of gunpowder and ozone, was a fractured tapestry of sound: the sharp clicks of agents securing the room, the low, angry shouts of Dimitri's men being cuffed, the crackle of a two-way radio giving orders. But for Finn, it all faded into a meaningless background hum. His world had shrunk to a single, agonizing point of light: Rhys.

He knelt on the cold concrete beside the cot, oblivious to the blood that slicked his knuckles and stained his clothes. His hands, which had just disarmed a man with brutal efficiency, were now a rough, clumsy shield around Rhys's face, his thumbs stroking the damp, pale skin of his cheeks. Rhys's body was a small, shaking vessel, wracked by a fresh wave of contractions that made him arch his back with a silent, desperate gasp. The scent of his pain, a potent, visceral perfume of fear and exertion, was the only thing Finn could smell, the only thing he could feel.

"Ramirez!" Finn's voice was a guttural command, stripped of all protocol, all professional deference.

Agent Ramirez, a formidable figure in her tactical vest, her face a mask of grim determination, moved toward them with a swift, purposeful stride. She knelt beside him, her gaze, sharp and analytical, taking in the scene: the defeated alpha, the shattered safe house, the bleeding man on the floor, and the omega in the throes of labor. Her hand, a steady, competent weight, came to rest on Rhys's forehead.

"The ledgers are secure," she said, her voice a low, no-nonsense murmur. "And a med-evac is inbound. Finn... you're going to be okay."

Finn's head, a heavy, bruised thing, simply shook. He wasn't okay. His body was a map of pain, his soul a ravaged battlefield. But he didn't care. His gaze, a fierce, protective fire, was fixed on Rhys. "The hospital. Now."

The journey was a blur of flashing red and blue lights, the siren a wailing banshee that sliced through the pre-dawn gloom of the city. The ambulance, a cramped, sterile box, smelled of antiseptic and ozone, a brutal contrast to the filth and decay of the safe house. Finn, his face a pale mask of exhaustion and pain, sat on the jump seat, his hand, a rough, calloused thing, never leaving Rhys's. He held it with a desperate, unyielding grip, a final, unshakeable tether in the storm.

Rhys's hand, a small, trembling thing, was a map of his own silent agony. His knuckles were white, his nails digging into Finn's palm, a raw, primal expression of a pain that was beyond words. He was a silent warrior, a quiet, defiant survivor who was now fighting the ultimate battle. Finn, his gaze fixed on his face, watched as the agony would seize him, his body arching, his face a mask of profound, unadulterated pain. And then, as the wave would recede, he would fall back against the gurney, his breath a short, sharp gasp, his eyes, a brilliant, terrifying blue, fixed on Finn's. In those moments, in the midst of the chaos, Finn saw him. The quiet, brilliant accountant. The lonely survivor. The brave, defiant omega who was now his everything.

The hospital was a world of sterile white and relentless, fluorescent light, a stark, clinical contrast to the gritty, rain-slicked streets of Chicago. The scent of antiseptic and clean linen was a cold, alien perfume. They were in a different world now, a world of life and hope, far from the brutal, unforgiving reality of the Petrov family.

Finn, his body a battlefield of bruises and cuts, his wounded side a throbbing, agonizing protest, was a phantom in this new world. He was a presence, a fierce, protective shadow, but he was a ghost. He stood in the corner of the room, his gaze a silent, fierce testament to his love, his hand never leaving Rhys's. He watched as the doctors, a blur of motion and crisp white coats, worked around him, their voices a low, professional murmur. He felt a deep, profound helplessness, a sensation he had not known since his earliest days as an agent. He was a protector whose own body had failed him, a guardian who was now a burden. But he was still there. He was still here.

The final push was a symphony of agony and triumph. Rhys's body, a small, trembling vessel of life, was a force of nature. He cried out, a low, guttural sound of pain and exertion, a sound that tore at Finn's heart. His hands, a small, desperate shield, pushed against the gurney, his face a mask of profound, unadulterated pain. And then, a new sound, a small, high-pitched wail, filled the room. The scent of new life, a fresh, clean, primal perfume of triumph, filled the air.

Finn, his body a magnificent, broken machine of muscle and bone, felt a profound, emotional tremor seize him. He looked at the doctors, at the small, pink, squirming bundle in their hands, and a sob, a deep, raw, guttural sound, tore from his throat. It was not a sound of pain, or of fear, but of profound, unadulterated relief. It was the sound of a man who had finally found his home.

The city, with its rain-slicked streets and its brutal, unforgiving rhythms, was a world away. Finn and Rhys, now a family, had moved to a quiet countryside home, a small, beautiful farm a few hundred miles from Chicago. The air, a clean, fresh perfume of pine and damp earth, was a brutal contrast to the acrid, polluted smell of the city. The sound of crickets, a gentle, rhythmic song, had replaced the wailing banshee of the sirens. The feel of soft, clean sheets on their skin, the scent of lavender and fresh-cut grass, was a brutal, beautiful contrast to the cold, sterile reality of their old life.

Finn was a different man. The agent, the shadow, the phantom in the machine—he was gone. He was a father now, his hands, once weapons of violence and survival, now a gentle, loving shield around his son. He would sit in the rocking chair, his son, a small, beautiful alpha, a sleeping bundle in his arms, and his gaze, a soft, loving fire, would be fixed on Rhys. The accountant, the survivor, the quiet, defiant omega—he was a mother now. He was a force of nature, a new, gentle, unyielding force of love and life.

The world had finally moved on. The Petrov family, a magnificent, terrifying beast, was gone. The ledgers, a silent, damning testament to their corruption, had been secured by Agent Ramirez. Finn, his name and reputation finally cleared, was officially exonerated. The FBI, forced to choose between their corrupt mole and the public outrage of the world, had chosen to dismantle the empire from the inside out. The ghost was finally free.

He and Rhys, now a family, were a world away. They had a home, a life, a future. They had their son, a beautiful, perfect testament to their love. They had a chance to build a new life, a life not built on lies and secrets, but on love and honesty.

One evening, as the sun, a magnificent, fiery orange orb, began to sink below the horizon, they sat on the porch, their hands intertwined. Their son, a sleeping bundle in Finn's arms, was a warm, beautiful weight against his chest. The sky, a beautiful, brutal canvas of a thousand shades of orange and red, was a final, magnificent display of a world moving on.

Finn looked at Rhys, at the quiet, beautiful man who had changed his life, who had made him a man, a father, a protector. He looked at their son, a perfect, beautiful reflection of their love. He smiled, a soft, quiet smile that reached his eyes, a smile that was not an agent's smile, but a man's. And in that moment, in the midst of the silence, in the gentle, loving embrace of the new night, he was finally home. The road ahead, a long, beautiful, and uncertain stretch of time, was finally theirs.

Thank you for reading—I truly hope you enjoyed the journey.
If you have a moment, a short review would mean the world. Even a sentence
helps others find their next great story, and your thoughts make a real
difference. Your support helps independent authors like me continue creating
the stories you love.

About the Author

Clara Throne is a versatile storyteller whose work spans the thrilling domains of crime, thriller, mystery, romance, and fantasy. With a career that has blossomed over two decades, she has become renowned for her razor-sharp plots and richly drawn characters that captivate readers across a spectrum of genres—from gritty crime thrillers to dark romance, from pulse-pounding psychological suspense to enchanting tales of forbidden love and fantastical realms.

Growing up surrounded by diverse landscapes and cultural influences, Clara discovered early on that every environment and human interaction contained stories waiting to be told. This innate curiosity propelled her into a lifelong pursuit of crafting narratives that blend the raw tension of a hard-hitting mystery with the tender intricacies of romance and the immersive depth of fantasy worlds. Her crime novels are marked by meticulously detailed investigations and morally complex protagonists, her romance thrillers pulse with emotional intensity and unexpected turns, and her fantasy works create rich, textured universes that readers can lose themselves in completely.

Clara's work has graced the pages of numerous literary journals and bestseller lists, earning her accolades from both readers and critics alike. With a diverse background that spans multiple disciplines including psychology, literature, and cultural studies, she brings authentic dimension to characters across all her genres. Her passion for weaving multifaceted stories has led her to explore narratives that defy traditional genre boundaries, resulting in a body of work that is both innovative and deeply resonant.

Whether unraveling a perplexing mystery in a sun-drenched coastal town, exploring the labyrinth of the human heart in a high-stakes corporate romance, diving into supernatural realms where reality bends to imagination, or crafting historical fiction where past and present collide, Clara Throne writes with clarity, passion, and an unwavering commitment to emotional truth. Her stories invite readers to step into worlds where connections form in the most unexpected circumstances, and where every ending opens the door to new possibilities.

Printed in Dunstable, United Kingdom